LOST HORIZON

◆ ◆ ◆

By Jan Christian Swoboda
Based on the novel by James Hilton

JAMES HILTON

for Julia

JAMES HILTON

LOST HORIZON

Dear Reader,

Have you ever dreamed of finding a perfect place? Not just a beautiful place, but somewhere that seems to exist outside of time itself - where the usual rush and worry of life fade away, and you can finally see what really matters? This is the story of such a place, and of the remarkable man who found it.

Our story begins with Hugh Conway, a British diplomat who, along with three other passengers, is evacuated from a revolution in a distant city. But their airplane is hijacked and taken far off course, eventually landing in the mysterious Himalayas - those great mountains that stretch like a wall across the roof of the world. There, hidden in a secret valley, they discover a place called Shangri-La.

When we first meet Conway, he seems like just another tired civil servant, doing his duty in far-off places. But as we learn his story, we discover someone far more interesting: a man who was changed by the Great War, who learned to look at the world differently, and who might just be ready to understand the deepest secrets of Shangri-La.

This isn't just an adventure story, though there is plenty of adventure. It's about the choices we all face between duty and happiness, between the life everyone expects us to live and the life we might choose if we dared. It's about how wisdom and beauty can survive in hidden places, waiting to be found by those who are ready to understand them. And it's about time itself - how it shapes us, changes us, and sometimes, in very special places, might work differently than we think.

As you read this story, you'll find yourself in a world that might seem very different from today. People travel by steamship instead of airplane, send telegrams instead of texts, and treat a journey to Tibet as something almost impossible. But you'll also find that many things haven't changed at all. People still search for meaning in their lives, still wonder if there might be more to the world than what we see every day, and still dream of finding perfect places.

Conway isn't perfect - he sometimes seems detached from life, unsure of his path, and haunted by his past. But that's what makes his journey to Shangri-La so important. Through his eyes, we get to explore not just a hidden monastery in the mountains, but the deeper questions that all of us face: What makes a life worthwhile? What should we preserve when the world seems to be falling apart? And what might we discover if we look beyond the ordinary world to find something extraordinary?

This adaptation aims to bring Conway's story to life for modern readers while keeping all the mystery and wonder of the original. Some descriptions have been enhanced, and some conversations expanded, but the heart of the story remains the same: one man's discovery of a place that challenges everything he thought he knew about life, time, and what really matters.

So come with us to Shangri-La. Walk through its peaceful courtyards, listen to its ancient music, and decide for yourself whether such a perfect place could really exist - or whether, perhaps, we need to believe it could.

Welcome to the Valley of the Blue Moon.

PROLOGUE

The three of us sat at an outdoor café near the Berlin airport, watching our cigarettes burn down as the evening grew awkward. It's funny how old school friends can meet up years later and find they don't have as much in common as they once thought. Rutherford was now a writer, Wyland worked at the British Embassy, and I was just passing through. Wyland had invited us to dinner at the Tempelhof Café—though he didn't seem too thrilled about it. I got the feeling that if we weren't all English guys living in a foreign city, we probably wouldn't have bothered meeting up at all.

I could tell that Wyland hadn't changed much since school—he was still kind of stuck-up, maybe even more so now that he had some fancy letters after his name. I liked Rutherford better; he'd grown up well from the skinny know-it-all kid I used to both pick on and look out for. The only thing Wyland and I seemed to share was a bit of jealousy, since Rutherford was probably making more money and having a way more interesting life than either of us.

But the evening wasn't boring, at least. We had an amazing view of the huge Luft-Hansa planes landing and taking off from all over Europe. As it got dark, they turned on these massive floodlights that made the whole scene look like something out of a movie. One of the planes was British, and its pilot walked past our table in full flying gear. He nodded at Wyland, who didn't recognize him at first. When he finally did, we all got introduced, and we invited the pilot—a friendly young guy named Sanders—to join us.

Wyland made some excuse about how hard it is to recognize people when they're all bundled up in flight suits and helmets. Sanders laughed and said, "Oh yeah, I totally get that. Remember what happened at Baskul?" Wyland gave a weird fake laugh, and quickly changed the subject.

Sanders turned out to be great company, and we all had quite a few beers together. Around ten o'clock, Wyland went to talk to someone at another table, and Rutherford turned to Sanders. "Hey, you mentioned Baskul earlier. I know that place a little. What were you talking about?"

Sanders smiled shyly at first but couldn't help himself from sharing the story. "Oh, just this crazy thing that happened when I was stationed there. Some guy—we think he was Afghan or from one of the local tribes—literally stole one of our planes. It was the most insane thing ever. He knocked out the pilot, took his uniform, and just walked right into the cockpit like he owned the place. Nobody even noticed! He even knew all the right signals to give the ground crew. Then he just took off and disappeared. The craziest part? He never came back."

Rutherford leaned forward, interested. "When did this happen?"

"Must've been about a year ago—May 2031. We were evacuating civilians from Baskul to Peshawur because of the revolution—you might remember hearing about it. The whole place was in chaos, which is probably the only reason someone could've pulled it off. Just goes to show how a uniform can make anyone look official, right?"

"I would've thought you'd have more than one person in charge of a plane during an evacuation," Rutherford said.

"We did, on all the regular planes. But this one was special—it was originally built for some maharajah, really fancy stuff. The Indian Survey team had been using it for high-altitude flights in Kashmir."

"And it never made it to Peshawur?"

"Nope. Never got there, and never crashed anywhere that we could find. That's the weird part. If the guy was from one of the local tribes, he might've headed for the mountains, thinking he could hold the passengers for ransom. I guess they all probably died somehow. There are tons of places up there where you could crash and never be found."

"How many passengers were on board?"

"Four, I think. Three men and a woman missionary."

"Was one of the men named Conway, by any chance?"

Sanders looked surprised. "Yeah, actually! 'Glory' Conway—did you know him?"

"We went to school together," Rutherford said, sounding a bit uncomfortable, like he didn't want to brag about the connection.

"He was incredible during the whole Baskul situation, from what I heard," Sanders added.

Rutherford nodded. "Yes, he definitely was... but how strange... really strange..." He seemed lost in thought for a moment, then said, "I never saw anything about this in the news. How come?"

Sanders suddenly looked uncomfortable, like he might have said too much. "Well, to be honest, I probably shouldn't have told you all this. Though I guess it doesn't matter now—everyone in the military knows about it, and it's all over the local gossip anyway. They kept it quiet, you see—I mean, the way it happened. Wouldn't have looked good. The government just announced that one of their planes was missing and listed the names. Not the kind of story that gets much attention from regular people."

Just then, Wyland came back and Sanders turned to him apologetically. "Hey, Wyland, we were just talking about 'Glory' Conway. I kind of spilled the beans about what happened at Baskul— hope that's okay?"

Wyland got all serious and quiet for a moment, like he was trying to decide between being polite to his countrymen and doing his official duty. Finally, he said, "I really wish you hadn't turned this into just another story. I thought you pilots were sworn to secrecy about these things." After scolding Sanders, he turned to Rutherford with a slightly nicer attitude. "Of course, it's different in your case, but I'm sure you understand that sometimes we need to keep things on the frontier a bit mysterious."

"On the other hand," Rutherford said dryly, "people tend to want to know the truth."

I was catching an early morning train across the continent, and as we waited for a taxi, Rutherford asked if I wanted to hang out at his hotel until then. He had a sitting room, he said, and we could talk. I said that would be perfect, and he replied: "Good. We can talk about Conway, if you want—unless you're totally sick of hearing about him."

I told him I wasn't sick of it at all, even though I had barely known

Conway. "He left school at the end of my first term, and I never saw him again. But he was incredibly kind to me once—I was the new kid, and there was no reason for him to do what he did. It was just a small thing, but I've never forgotten it."

"Yeah, I liked him a lot too," Rutherford said, "though I also didn't spend much time with him, if you really count it up."

Then there was this weird silence, where it was clear we were both thinking about someone who had meant a lot more to us than you'd expect from such brief encounters. I've often noticed since then that other people who met Conway, even just once or briefly, remembered him really clearly. He was definitely remarkable as a teenager, and to me, back when I was at that age where you look up to older students, my memory of him is still almost legendary. He was tall and really good-looking, and not only was he great at sports, but he won every kind of academic prize too. Our kind of sentimental headmaster once called his achievements 'glorious,' and that became his nickname. Probably only Conway could have pulled off having a nickname like that. I remember he gave a graduation speech in ancient Greek, and he was amazing in school plays. There was something almost Renaissance-man-like about him—how he could do everything well, his good looks, that amazing combination of being both smart and athletic. Like a modern-day Sir Philip Sidney. You don't see people like that much anymore.

I said something like this to Rutherford, and he replied: "Yeah, that's true, and we have a special word we use to put down people like that nowadays—we call them 'jack of all trades.' I bet some people called Conway that—people like Wyland, for instance. I don't much care for Wyland. I can't stand his type—all that properness and self-importance. And that total head prefect mentality—did you notice? Little phrases about 'sworn to secrecy' and 'telling tales out of school'—like running the British Empire is the same as being a hall monitor! But then again, I never get along with these diplomat types."

We drove a few blocks in silence, and then he continued: "Still, I'm glad I came tonight. It was weird for me, hearing Sanders tell that story about what happened at Baskul. You see, I'd heard it before, but I hadn't really believed it. It was part of an even more incredible story that I had no reason to believe at all—well, just one tiny reason, anyway. Now there are two tiny reasons. I should tell you that I'm not exactly gullible. I've traveled a lot, and I know there are strange things in the world—if you see them yourself, that is, but not so often if you just hear about them secondhand. And yet..."

He suddenly seemed to realize that what he was saying probably didn't make much sense to me, and he laughed. "Well, one thing's for sure—I'm definitely not going to tell Wyland about it. It would be like trying to sell a fantasy novel to a technical manual publisher. I'd rather try my luck with you."

"Maybe you're giving me too much credit," I suggested.

"Your book makes me think I'm not."

I hadn't mentioned that I'd written that pretty technical book (after all, not everyone's interested in neurology), and I was pleasantly surprised that Rutherford had even heard of it. I said as much, and he answered: "Well, you see, I was interested because memory loss was Conway's problem—at one point."

We had reached his hotel and needed to get his key from the front desk. As we rode the elevator to the fifth floor, he dropped a bombshell: "The thing is, Conway isn't dead. At least, he wasn't a few months ago."

This was way too big to process in the short elevator ride. In the hallway, I finally managed to ask, "Are you sure about that? How do you know?"

He waited until he'd unlocked his door to answer: "Because I traveled with him from Shanghai to Honolulu on a Japanese cruise ship last November." He didn't say anything else until we were settled in armchairs with drinks. "See, I was in China last fall—on vacation. I travel a lot. I hadn't seen Conway in years—we never kept in touch, but his was one of those faces I could always picture perfectly if I tried. I had been visiting a friend in Hankow and was taking the Peking Express back. On the train, I started chatting with this really nice French nun who was the Mother Superior of a charity hospital. She was heading to Chung-Kiang where her convent was, and since I spoke a little French, she seemed happy to tell me about her work and stuff.

"To be honest, I'm not usually big on missionary work, but I have to admit the Catholic ones are different—they actually work hard and don't act all superior about it. Anyway, that's beside the point. The important thing is that this nun, while telling me about their hospital in Chung-Kiang, mentioned this weird fever case they'd gotten a few weeks back—a man they thought must be European, but he couldn't tell them anything about himself and had no ID. His clothes were local and super poor quality, and when the nuns found him, he'd been really sick. He spoke perfect Chinese, good French, and the nun told me that before he realized they were French, he'd spoken to them in perfect English with what she called a 'refined accent.' I joked with her about how she could tell it was refined when she didn't even speak English. We laughed about that and other things, and she ended up inviting me to visit if I was ever in the area. At the time, this seemed about as likely as me climbing Mount Everest, and when we got to Chung-Kiang, I said goodbye, honestly sad that our random meeting was over.

"But here's where it gets weird—I ended up back in Chung-Kiang just hours later. The train broke down a couple miles ahead, and they had to push us back to the station. We found out we'd be stuck there for at least twelve hours waiting for a replacement engine. That's pretty normal for Chinese railways. So I had half a day to kill in Chung-Kiang —which made me think, why not take the nun up on her offer and visit the mission?

"I did, and they were really surprised but super welcoming. I guess one thing non-Catholics don't always get is how Catholics can be totally strict about official stuff but super chill about everything else. Is that too complicated? Anyway, doesn't matter—those mission people were great company. Before I knew it, they'd made me lunch, and this young Chinese doctor who was also Christian sat with me and we had this fun conversation in a mix of French and English. After that, he and the Mother Superior showed me around the hospital, which they were really proud of. I'd told them I was a writer, and they got all excited thinking I might put them in a book. We were walking past the beds while the doctor explained each case. The place was super clean and seemed really well-run. I'd actually forgotten about the mysterious patient with the fancy English accent until the Mother Superior reminded me as we were approaching his bed. All I could see was the back of his head; he seemed to be sleeping. She suggested I say something in English, so I just said 'Good afternoon,' because that was the first thing that came to mind.

"The man looked up suddenly and said 'Good afternoon' back. And you know what? His accent really was educated. But I didn't have time to be surprised about that, because I'd already recognized him—even with his beard and totally different appearance and all the years since we'd last met. It was Conway. I was absolutely certain it was, even though if I'd stopped to think about it, I probably would've convinced myself it couldn't possibly be him. Luckily, I just went with my gut. I called out his name and mine, and even though he looked at me without any sign that he knew who I was, I was positive I hadn't made a mistake. There was this weird little twitch in his face muscles that I remembered from before, and he had the same eyes that at school we used to joke were more Cambridge blue than Oxford blue. But besides all that, he was just one of those people you couldn't mistake—once you'd seen him, you'd know him anywhere.

"Of course, the doctor and the Mother Superior got super excited. I told them that I knew this man, that he was English, and that he was my friend, and if he didn't recognize me, it must be because he'd completely lost his memory. They nodded, kind of amazed, and we had a long talk about his case. They had no idea how Conway could have possibly ended up in Chung-Kiang in that condition.

"Long story short, I stayed there for over two weeks, hoping I could somehow help him remember things. I didn't succeed in bringing his memory back, but his physical health improved, and we talked a lot. When I told him straight-up who I was and who he was, he was cool about not arguing with it. He was even kind of cheerful, in a vague sort of way, and seemed happy enough to have me around. When I suggested taking him home, he just said he didn't mind. It was kind of unsettling, that lack of any personal preference. As soon as I could, I arranged for us to leave. I confided in someone I knew at the British consulate in Hankow, which helped us get the necessary passport and paperwork without too much fuss. I figured that for Conway's sake, we should keep this whole thing quiet, away from news headlines and media attention—and I'm glad to say I managed that. The press would have had a field day with it.

"We left China pretty normally. We took a boat down the Yangtze River to Nanking, then caught a train to Shanghai. There was a Japanese ship leaving for San Francisco that same night, so we made a mad dash and got on board."

"You did a lot for him," I said.

Rutherford didn't deny it. "I probably wouldn't have done that much for anyone else," he admitted. "But there was something about him, always had been—it's hard to explain, but it made you want to help him."

"Yeah," I agreed. "He had this special charm, this likeable quality that's nice to remember even now—though of course, I still picture him as a kid in cricket clothes."

"Too bad you didn't know him at Oxford. He was just brilliant—there's no other word for it. After the war, people said he was different—I think he was. But I can't help feeling that with all his talents, he should have been doing bigger things—all that diplomatic service stuff wasn't what I'd expect from someone truly great. And Conway was—or should have been—great. You and I both knew him, and I don't think I'm exaggerating when I say it's an experience we'll never forget. And even when he and I met in the middle of China, with his mind blank and his past a mystery, he still had that weird core of... something special about him.

"As you can imagine, we rebuilt our old friendship on the ship. I told him everything I knew about who he was, and he listened so carefully it almost seemed funny. He remembered everything clearly since arriving at Chung-Kiang, and get this—he hadn't forgotten languages. He told me he knew he must have had something to do with India because he could speak Hindi.

"In Yokohama, more passengers got on, including this famous pianist named Sieveking who was heading to America for a concert tour. He sat at our dining table and sometimes talked with Conway in German. That shows you how normal Conway seemed on the outside. Apart from his memory loss, which didn't show in regular conversation, you wouldn't have thought anything was wrong with him.

"A few nights after leaving Japan, Sieveking agreed to give a piano concert on board, and Conway and I went to listen. He played really well—some Brahms, Scarlatti, and lots of Chopin. I glanced at Conway a couple times and could tell he was enjoying it, which made sense given his own musical background. After the main program, it turned into this informal encore session where Sieveking—pretty nicely, I thought—played more pieces for some fans gathered around the piano. He mostly played more Chopin—that's kind of his specialty. Finally, he left the piano and headed for the door, still followed by admirers, clearly feeling he'd done enough for them. But then something weird started happening. Conway had sat down at the keyboard and was playing this fast, lively piece that Sieveking didn't recognize. Sieveking came rushing back, super excited, asking what it was. Conway, after this long, strange silence, could only say he didn't know. Sieveking said that was impossible and got even more excited. Conway then seemed to make this huge physical and mental effort to remember, and finally said it was a Chopin study. I didn't think it was, and I wasn't surprised when Sieveking absolutely denied it. But then Conway got suddenly really worked up about it—which shocked me because until then he'd been so emotionless about everything. 'Listen,' Sieveking argued, 'I know every single thing Chopin ever wrote, and I can promise you that what you just played isn't one of them. It totally could be—it's exactly his style—but it just isn't. I dare you to show me where to find it in any published version.'

"And Conway answered: 'Oh yeah, I remember now—it was never published. I only know it because I met someone who used to be one of Chopin's students... Here's another unpublished piece I learned from him.'"

Rutherford gave me a meaningful look before continuing: "Now, even if you're not into music, you can probably imagine how mind-blowing this was for Sieveking, and for me too. For me, it was suddenly this mysterious glimpse into Conway's lost past—the first clue of any kind we'd gotten. Sieveking was fascinated by the musical puzzle—which was pretty wild, considering Chopin died in 1849.

"This whole incident was so bizarre that I should probably mention there were at least a dozen witnesses—including a well-known California university professor. Sure, it was easy to say that Conway's explanation was basically impossible, but then how do you explain the music itself? If it wasn't what Conway said it was, then what was it? Sieveking told me that if those two pieces were ever published, every serious pianist in the world would be playing them within six months. Even if that's an exaggeration, it shows what Sieveking thought of them. After arguing about it for a while, we couldn't figure anything out, because Conway stuck to his story, and since he was starting to look tired, I wanted to get him away from the crowd and into bed. The last thing we talked about was making some recordings. Sieveking said he'd set everything up once we got to America, and Conway promised to play for the microphone. Looking back, it's really too bad he never got the chance to keep that promise.

"Because that night—the night after the recital—his memory came back. We'd both gone to bed and I was lying awake when he came into my cabin and told me. His face had frozen into this expression of... I can only call it overwhelming sadness—but not just personal sadness, more like sadness for the whole world, if that makes any sense. He said he could remember everything now, that it had started coming back during Sieveking's playing, though only in pieces at first. He sat for a long time on the edge of my bed, and I let him take his time and tell it his own way. I said I was glad his memory was back but sorry if he already wished it wasn't. He looked up then and paid me what I'll always think of as an amazing compliment. 'Thank God, Rutherford,' he said, 'you can actually imagine things.'

"After a while I got dressed and convinced him to do the same, and we walked up and down the boat deck. It was a calm night, starry and really warm, and the sea looked weirdly pale and thick, like condensed milk. Except for the engines vibrating, we might have been walking in a park. I let Conway go at his own pace, without questions at first. Somewhere around dawn he started telling the story in order, and it was mid-morning and blazing hot when he finished. When I say 'finished,' I don't mean there wasn't more to tell me after that first confession. He filled in quite a few important gaps during the next twenty-four hours. He was really unhappy and couldn't have slept, so we talked almost non-stop. About halfway through the following night, the ship was supposed to reach Honolulu. We had drinks in my cabin the evening before; he left around ten o'clock, and I never saw him again."

"You don't mean—" I pictured someone calmly jumping overboard.

Rutherford laughed. "Oh no, nothing like that—he wasn't that type. He just ditched me. It was pretty easy to get off the ship, but he must have had a hard time avoiding being found when I got people searching for him, which of course I did. Later I found out he'd managed to get a job on a banana boat heading south to Fiji."

"How did you find that out?"

"Pretty straightforwardly. He wrote to me, three months later, from Bangkok. He sent money to cover all the expenses I'd paid for him. He thanked me and said he was feeling great. He also said he was about to start a long journey—to the northwest. That was all."

"Where was he heading?"

"Yeah, it's pretty vague, right? Lots of places lie northwest of Bangkok. Even Berlin does, technically."

Rutherford paused and refilled our glasses. It had been a strange story —or maybe he'd just made it seem that way; I wasn't sure which. The music part was puzzling, but what interested me more was the mystery of how Conway had ended up at that Chinese mission hospital; and I said so. Rutherford answered that they were actually both parts of the same puzzle. "Well, how did he get to Chung-Kiang?" I asked. "I assume he told you everything that night on the ship?"

"He told me something about it, and it would be silly of me, after telling you this much, to get secretive about the rest. It's just that, first of all, it's a pretty long story, and there wouldn't be time to even outline it before you'd have to catch your train. And besides, as it happens, there's an easier way. I know it's kind of embarrassing to reveal the tricks of my questionable profession, but the truth is, Conway's story, as I thought about it afterward, really grabbed me. I'd started by taking simple notes after our various conversations on the ship, so I wouldn't forget details; later, as certain aspects of the thing started to fascinate me, I felt compelled to do more—to shape all the written and remembered pieces into one complete narrative. By that I don't mean I made anything up or changed anything. There was plenty of material in what he told me—he was good at telling stories and had a natural talent for creating atmosphere. Also, I guess I felt I was starting to understand the man himself." He went to his briefcase and took out a stack of typed papers. "Well, here it is, anyway, and you can make what you want of it."

"Which I guess means you don't expect me to believe it?"

"Oh, not quite such a strong warning as that. But remember, if you do believe it, it'll be for that famous reason Tertullian gave—'because it is impossible.' Not a bad argument, maybe. Let me know what you think, anyway."

I took the manuscript with me and read most of it on the train to Ostend. I planned to return it with a long letter when I got to England, but there were delays, and before I could mail it, I got a short note from Rutherford saying he was off traveling again and wouldn't have a fixed address for several months. He was going to Kashmir, he wrote, and from there "east." I wasn't surprised.

CHAPTER 1

By the third week of May, things in Baskul had gotten really bad. On the 20th, the Air Force sent planes from Peshawur to evacuate all the Western residents. There were about eighty people to rescue, and most of them got safely transported across the mountains in military transport planes. They also used a few other aircraft, including this fancy private plane borrowed from the Maharajah of Chandapore. Around 10 AM, four passengers got on board: Miss Roberta Brinklow from the Eastern Mission, Henry D. Barnard (an American), Hugh Conway (the British Consul), and Captain Charles Mallinson (the Vice-Consul).

These were the names that would later appear in the Indian and British news.

Conway was thirty-seven. He'd been working in Baskul for two years, in what now looked like a losing bet. This chapter of his life was over; in a few weeks, or maybe after a vacation in England, they'd send him somewhere else. Tokyo or Tehran, Manila or Muscat—in his line of work, you never knew where you'd end up next. After ten years in the Consular Service, he knew exactly where he stood career-wise, just like he could size up anyone else's chances. He knew he wouldn't get the cushiest jobs, but he actually found that comforting rather than disappointing. He preferred the more interesting, less formal positions, and since these weren't usually considered the "good" jobs, others probably thought he was making bad career moves.

But for his own happiness, he felt he'd played his cards just right —he'd had an interesting and pretty enjoyable ten years.

He was tall and deeply tanned, with short brown hair and slate-blue eyes. He usually looked serious and thoughtful until he laughed, and then (which didn't happen too often) he looked like a kid again. He had this small nervous twitch near his left eye that showed up when he worked too hard or drank too much. Since he'd spent the entire day and night before the evacuation packing and destroying documents, the twitch was really obvious when he climbed into the plane. He was exhausted and incredibly grateful that he'd managed to get a spot on the maharajah's luxury aircraft instead of one of the packed military transports. He settled into the comfortable seat as the plane took off. He was the kind of person who, being used to major hardships, expected small comforts to make up for it. He'd happily rough it on the road to Samarkand, but he'd spend his last dollar on first class for a trip from London to Paris.

They'd been flying for over an hour when Mallinson said he thought the pilot wasn't keeping to the right course. Mallinson sat right in front. He was in his mid-twenties, with rosy cheeks and quick intelligence, though he wasn't exactly an intellectual. He had all the typical limitations of someone from an elite British school, but also all the good qualities. He'd been sent to Baskul because he failed an exam, and Conway had worked with him for six months and grown to like him.

But Conway didn't feel like making the effort that talking on a plane requires. He opened his eyes sleepily and said that whatever route they were taking, the pilot probably knew what he was doing.

Half an hour later, just when tiredness and the drone of the engine had almost put him to sleep, Mallinson bothered him again. "Hey, Conway, I thought Fenner was supposed to be flying us?"

"Well, isn't he?"

"The guy just turned his head and I swear it wasn't him."

"It's hard to tell through that glass panel."

"I'd know Fenner's face anywhere."

"Well, then it must be someone else. I don't see why it matters."

"But Fenner specifically told me he was taking this plane."

"They must have changed their minds and given him one of the others."

"Well, who is this guy, then?"

"How should I know? You don't think I've memorized the face of every Air Force pilot, do you?"

"I know quite a few of them, but I don't recognize this one."

"Then he must be one of the many you don't know." Conway smiled and added: "When we get to Peshawur soon, you can introduce yourself and ask him all about himself."

"At this rate we won't get to Peshawur at all. The guy's completely off course. And I'm not surprised—he's flying so high he can't even see where he's going."

Conway wasn't worried. He was used to flying and didn't fuss about details. Besides, there wasn't anything special waiting for him in Peshawur, no one he was particularly excited to see, so he didn't care if the trip took four hours or six. He was single; there wouldn't be any emotional welcomes when they landed. He had friends, and some of them would probably take him to the club for drinks—a nice prospect, but nothing to get worked up about.

He didn't get worked up looking back at the past decade either. Changeable, some good times, getting a bit unstable—that had been true for both his life and the world in general. He thought about Baskul, Beijing, Macau, and all the other places—he'd moved around quite a bit. Farthest back was Oxford, where he'd spent a couple of years teaching after the war, giving lectures on Asian History, breathing in dusty library air, riding his bike down the High Street. He liked remembering it, but it didn't stir up strong emotions; somehow he felt like he was still connected to all the different lives he could have lived.

A familiar lurch in his stomach told him the plane was starting to descend. He felt like teasing Mallinson about all his worrying, and might have done it if the younger man hadn't suddenly jumped up, hitting his head on the roof and waking up Barnard, the American, who had been dozing in his seat across the narrow aisle. "Oh my God!" Mallinson shouted, looking out the window. "Look down there!"

Conway looked. What he saw was definitely not what he'd expected—if he'd been expecting anything specific. Instead of the neat, geometric layout of the military base and the big rectangular hangars, all he could see was a thick mist covering what looked like an endless, sun-baked wasteland. The plane was coming down fast but was still flying way higher than normal. He could make out long, ridged mountain ranges maybe a mile closer than the hazier valleys below. It was typical Frontier scenery, though Conway had never seen it from this high up before. It was also—which struck him as strange—nowhere he recognized near Peshawur. "I don't know this part of the world," he said. Then, more quietly, so as not to worry the others, he added to Mallinson: "Looks like you're right—the guy's lost."

The plane was diving down at incredible speed, and as it descended, the air got hotter; the scorched earth below was like opening an oven door. One mountain peak after another appeared on the horizon, jagged against the sky. Now they were flying along a curved valley scattered with rocks and dried-up river beds. It looked like a floor covered in nutshells. The plane bounced and jerked in air pockets as roughly as a rowboat in choppy water. All four passengers had to hold onto their seats.

"Looks like he's going to land!" the American shouted hoarsely.

"He can't!" Mallinson shot back. "He'd be crazy to try! He'll crash and then—"

But the pilot did land. A small cleared space appeared beside a ravine, and with impressive skill, he bounced and wrestled the plane to a stop. What happened next, though, was even more puzzling and definitely not reassuring. A crowd of bearded men in turbans seemed to appear from nowhere, surrounding the plane and making it impossible for anyone to get out except the pilot. He climbed down and had an excited conversation with them, during which it became very clear that not only was he not Fenner, he wasn't even English, and maybe not even European. Meanwhile, they brought gas cans from a nearby cache and filled up the plane's unusually large tanks. The four trapped passengers' shouts were met with grins and silence, and any attempt to get out was stopped by a threatening wave of rifles. Conway, who knew a little of the local language, tried talking to the tribesmen, but it didn't help. The pilot's only response to anyone speaking to him in any language was to wave his gun meaningfully. The midday sun blazing on the cabin roof turned it into an oven, and the passengers were nearly passing out from the heat and from yelling their protests. They were completely helpless; one of the evacuation rules had been that they couldn't carry any weapons.

When they finally finished filling the tanks, someone passed a gas can filled with warm water through one of the cabin windows. They wouldn't answer any questions, though the men didn't seem personally hostile. After more discussion, the pilot climbed back into the cockpit, one of the local men awkwardly spun the propeller, and they took off again. Getting airborne from that tiny space with all the extra fuel was even more impressive than the landing had been. The plane climbed high into the hazy air, then turned east, as if following some plan. It was mid-afternoon.

It was the most bizarre and confusing thing any of them had ever experienced! As the cooler air refreshed them, they could hardly believe it had actually happened. No one could think of anything like it ever happening before in all the wild history of the Frontier. It would have been unbelievable if they weren't experiencing it themselves. Naturally, they went from disbelief to intense anger, and only started trying to figure it out once their anger wore off. Mallinson came up with a theory that, lacking any better explanation, they all found easiest to accept: They were being kidnapped for ransom. The trick wasn't new itself, though this particular method was definitely original. It was slightly comforting to think they weren't making completely new history; after all, kidnappings had happened before, and many of them had turned out okay. The tribesmen would keep you in some mountain hideout until the government paid up and you were released. You were treated decently enough, and since it wasn't your own money being paid, the whole thing was only unpleasant while it lasted. Afterward, of course, the Air Force would send bombers, and you'd have an amazing story to tell for the rest of your life. Mallinson explained this theory a bit nervously, but Barnard, the American, tried to make jokes about it.

"Well, folks, I guess this is a clever idea on somebody's part, but I can't say your Air Force comes out looking too good. You Brits make fun of hijackings in Chicago and all that, but I don't remember anyone ever stealing one of Uncle Sam's planes. And by the way, I'd like to know what this guy did with the real pilot. Knocked him out, I bet." He yawned. He was a big, heavy-set man with a weathered face where laugh lines competed with worried wrinkles. Nobody in Baskul had known much about him except that he'd come from Persia, where they assumed he worked in oil.

Meanwhile, Conway was doing something practical. He'd collected every scrap of paper they all had and was writing emergency messages in various local languages to drop from the plane. It was a tiny chance, in such empty country, but worth trying.

The fourth passenger, Miss Brinklow, sat straight-backed and tight-lipped, making few comments and no complaints. She was a small, tough-looking woman who seemed like someone forced to attend a party where things were happening that she didn't quite approve of.

Conway had talked less than the other two men because translating SOS messages into different languages took concentration. He had answered questions when asked, though, and had cautiously agreed with Mallinson's kidnapping theory. He'd also somewhat agreed with Barnard's criticism of the Air Force. "Though you can see how it might have happened," he said. "With everything in chaos like it was, one guy in flying gear would look pretty much like another. Nobody would question someone who looked like they knew what they were doing and wore the right uniform. And this guy obviously knows his stuff —the signals and everything. Pretty clear he knows how to fly too... but I agree someone's probably going to get in big trouble for this. And someone will, for sure, though I bet it won't be whoever really deserves it."

"Well, sir," Barnard replied, "I sure do admire how you can see both sides of things. That's probably the right attitude, even when you're being taken for a ride."

Conway thought about how Americans had this knack for

saying condescending things without being offensive. He smiled tolerantly but didn't continue the conversation. His exhaustion was the kind that even possible danger couldn't keep at bay. Later in the afternoon, when Barnard and Mallinson, who'd been arguing, asked his opinion about something, they found he'd fallen asleep.

"Totally exhausted," Mallinson said. "And I don't blame him, after these last few weeks."

"You know him well?" Barnard asked.

"I've worked with him at the Consulate. I happen to know he hasn't slept in four days. Actually, we're really lucky to have him with us in a mess like this. Besides knowing the languages, he has this way of dealing with people. If anyone can get us out of this situation, it'll be him. He stays pretty cool about most things."

"Well, let him sleep then," Barnard agreed.

Miss Brinklow made one of her rare comments. "I think he looks like a very brave man," she said.

Conway was far less sure that he was a very brave man. He had closed his eyes from pure physical exhaustion, but he wasn't really sleeping. He could hear and feel every movement of the plane, and he also heard, with mixed feelings, Mallinson praising him. That's when he had his doubts, recognizing the tight feeling in his stomach that came whenever he had to face an uncomfortable truth about himself. He knew from experience that he wasn't one of those people who loved danger for its own sake. There was one part of it he sometimes enjoyed—the excitement, the way it shook you out of feeling bored or numb—but he was definitely not fond of risking his life. During World War I, twelve years earlier, he'd grown to hate the dangers of trench warfare in France, and had several times avoided death by refusing to attempt heroic but impossible tasks. Even his Distinguished Service Order medal had been won more through his ability to endure than through physical courage. And since the War, whenever he'd faced danger again, he'd liked it less and less unless it promised some really extraordinary thrills to make it worthwhile.

He kept his eyes closed. He felt touched, and a little uncomfortable, hearing what Mallinson had said. It was his fate in life to have people mistake his calmness for courage—when actually it was something much less emotional and much less manly. They were all in an incredibly difficult situation, he thought, and far from feeling brave about it, he mainly felt a huge reluctance to deal with whatever trouble was coming. There was Miss Brinklow, for instance. He could see that in certain situations, he'd have to act as if she mattered more than all the rest of them put together just because she was a woman, and he dreaded having to make that kind of unfair choice.

Still, when he showed signs of waking up, it was to Miss Brinklow that he spoke first. He was glad to notice she was neither young nor pretty—negative qualities, but really helpful in the kind of trouble they might find themselves in. He also felt a bit sorry for her, because he suspected that neither Mallinson nor the American liked missionaries, especially female ones. He himself didn't have any prejudices, but he worried she might find his open-mindedness even more confusing than their dislike. "We seem to be in a strange situation," he said, leaning forward to speak quietly to her, "but I'm glad you're staying calm.

I don't really think anything terrible is going to happen to us."

"I'm sure it won't if you can prevent it," she answered, which didn't make him feel any better.

"Please let me know if there's anything we can do to make you more comfortable."

Barnard caught the word. "Comfortable?" he laughed loudly. "Why, of course we're comfortable. We're just enjoying the trip. Too bad we don't have any cards—we could play bridge."

Conway appreciated the attempt at humor, though he didn't like bridge. "I don't suppose Miss Brinklow plays," he said with a smile.

But the missionary turned around quickly to reply: "Actually, I do, and I never saw anything wrong with cards at all. There's nothing against them in the Bible."

They all laughed, grateful to her for giving them a reason to. At least, Conway thought, she wasn't hysterical.

All afternoon the plane had soared through the thin mists of the upper atmosphere, way too high to see clearly what was below. Sometimes, with long gaps in between, the mist would tear open for a moment to show the jagged edge of a mountain peak or the glint of some unknown river. They could figure out roughly which way they were going from the sun; they were still heading east, with occasional turns to the north. But where exactly they'd ended up depended on how fast they'd been flying, which

Conway couldn't judge accurately. It seemed likely, though, that they must have used up quite a lot of fuel by now—but that too depended on things he wasn't sure about. Conway didn't know much about planes technically, but he was certain that whoever the pilot was, he was definitely an expert. That landing in the rocky valley had proved it, along with other things he'd done since. And Conway couldn't help feeling what he always felt when he encountered any kind of undeniable expertise: a kind of respect. He was so used to people coming to him for help that just being aware of someone who neither needed nor wanted his help was oddly calming, even with all the worries about what might happen next. But he didn't expect the others to share such a subtle feeling. He knew they probably had much more personal reasons to be anxious than he did. Mallinson, for instance, was engaged to a girl in England; Barnard might be married; Miss Brinklow had her mission work, or however she thought of it. Mallinson, particularly, was by far the most stressed out; as time passed, he got more and more worked up—and even started criticizing to Conway's face the very calmness he'd praised behind his back.

At one point, above the roar of the engine, a heated argument broke out. "Look here," Mallinson shouted angrily, "are we just going to sit here twiddling our thumbs while this lunatic does whatever he wants? What's stopping us from breaking through that panel and dealing with him?"

"Nothing at all," Conway replied, "except that he has a gun and we don't, and also that none of us would know how to land the plane afterward."

"It can't be that hard, surely. I bet you could do it."

"My dear Mallinson, why do you always expect me to perform these miracles?"

"Well, this whole thing is really getting on my nerves. Can't we make him come down?"

"How do you suggest we do that?"

Mallinson was getting more and more agitated. "Well, he's right there, isn't he? About six feet away, and we're three men against one! Do we have to just stare at his back the whole time? We could at least force him to tell us what's going on."

"Alright, we'll see." Conway walked forward to the partition between the cabin and the pilot's cockpit, which was in front and slightly higher up. There was a glass panel, about six inches square that could slide open, through which the pilot could turn his head and bend down slightly to talk to his passengers. Conway knocked on it. What happened next was almost funny in how predictable it was. The glass panel slid open and a gun barrel poked through. No words, just that. Conway backed away without arguing, and the panel slid shut again.

Mallinson, who'd watched this happen, wasn't entirely convinced. "I don't think he would've actually shot," he said. "He's probably bluffing."

"Quite possibly," Conway agreed, "but I'd rather let you be the one to test that theory."

"Well, I just feel we ought to put up some kind of fight instead of just giving in like this."

Conway understood where he was coming from. He recognized the idea, with all its connections to stories about red-coated soldiers and school history books, that Englishmen never fear anything, never surrender, and never lose. He said: "Starting a fight when you have no real chance of winning is a bad move, and I'm not that kind of hero."

"Good for you, sir," Barnard chimed in heartily. "When somebody's got you cornered, you might as well accept it gracefully and admit it. I'm going to enjoy life while I can and have a cigar. I hope you don't mind a little extra danger, Miss Brinklow?"

"Not at all," she answered politely. "I don't smoke myself, but I just love the smell of cigars."

Conway thought she was exactly the type of woman who would say something like that. At least Mallinson had calmed down a bit, and to show there were no hard feelings, Conway offered him a cigarette, though he didn't light one himself. "I know how you feel," he said gently. "It's a bad situation, and in some ways it's worse because there's not much we can do about it."

'And better in other ways,' he couldn't help adding to himself. Because he was still incredibly tired. There was also something in his nature that some people might have called laziness, though it wasn't quite that. No one could work harder when it was necessary, and few people could handle responsibility better; but the fact was he didn't particularly love being active, and he definitely didn't enjoy being responsible. Both were part of his job, and he made the best of them, but he was always happy to let someone else take over if they could do it as well or better. This was partly why his career hadn't been as impressive as it might have been. He wasn't ambitious enough to push past others, or to make a big show of doing nothing when there was really nothing to do. His official reports were sometimes so brief they were almost rude, and while people admired his calmness in emergencies, they often suspected it wasn't quite proper. Authority likes to feel that someone is making an effort to stay calm, that their apparent coolness is just hiding a proper set of appropriate emotions. With Conway, people sometimes suspected that he really was as unruffled as he seemed, and that whatever happened, he genuinely didn't care that much. But this, like the apparent laziness, wasn't quite right either. What most people failed to see in him was something incredibly simple—he just loved quiet, thinking, and being alone.

Now, since that's what he felt like doing and there was nothing else to do anyway, he leaned back in his chair and properly fell asleep. When he woke up, he noticed that despite all their various worries, the others had done the same. Miss Brinklow was sitting perfectly straight with her eyes closed, like some old-fashioned statue; Mallinson had slumped forward with his chin in his hand. The American was even snoring. Very sensible of them all, Conway thought; there was no point wearing themselves out with shouting. But then he became aware of some odd physical sensations—slight dizziness, his heart pounding, and having to breathe deeply with effort. He remembered feeling similar things once before—in Switzerland.

Then he turned to the window and looked out. The sky around them had completely cleared, and in the late afternoon light, he saw something that literally took his breath away. Far in the distance, at the very edge of what he could see, was range after range of snow-covered mountain peaks, decorated with glaciers, floating like they were suspended on vast layers of clouds. They stretched all the way around in a circle, blending into a western horizon that was so intensely colored it looked like some mad genius's painting. And there in the middle of this incredible scene, their plane droned on over an endless drop, facing a sheer white wall that seemed to be part of the sky itself until the sun hit it. Then, like a dozen Swiss Alps stacked on top of each other, it burst into dazzling, brilliant white fire.

Conway wasn't usually easily impressed, and generally didn't care for 'views'—especially the famous ones where helpful city planners put benches for tourists. Once, when someone took him to Tiger Hill near Darjeeling to watch the sunrise on Mount Everest, he'd found the highest mountain in the world kind of disappointing. But this terrifying sight outside his window was different; it wasn't trying to be admired. There was something raw and monstrous about those harsh ice cliffs, and something incredibly daring about approaching them like this. He thought carefully, picturing maps, calculating distances, estimating times and speeds. Then he realized Mallinson had woken up too. He touched the young man's arm.

All they could do now was stare in wonder—and worry—at where their mysterious journey was taking them.

CHAPTER 2

It was just like Conway to let the others wake up on their own and not make a big deal about their shocked reactions to the view. Later, when Barnard asked what he thought about their situation, he explained it like a professor calmly solving a puzzle. He thought they were probably still in India, he said. They'd been flying east for several hours, too high to see much, but likely following some river valley that ran east to west. "I wish I had a map," he said, "but from what I remember, the upper Indus Valley would fit what we've seen. That would put us in one of the most spectacular places on Earth—and as you can see, that's exactly where we are."

"So you know where we are?" Barnard cut in.

"Well, no—I've never actually been anywhere near here before, but I wouldn't be surprised if that mountain is Nanga Parbat —the one where the famous climber Mummery died. From everything I've heard about it, the shape and layout match."

"You're a mountain climber?"

"I used to be pretty into it when I was younger. Just the usual Swiss Alps stuff, though."

Mallinson broke in irritably: "It'd be more useful to talk about where we're going. I wish someone could tell us that."

"Well, looks to me like we're heading for that mountain range up ahead," said Barnard. "Don't you think so, Conway? Hope you don't mind me using your first name, but if we're all going to have an adventure together, seems silly to be too formal."

Conway thought it was perfectly natural for someone to use his name and found Barnard's apology unnecessary. "Of course," he agreed, adding, "I think that range must be the Karakorams. There are several mountain passes if our pilot plans to cross them."

"Our pilot?" Mallinson exclaimed. "You mean our crazy kidnapper! We should forget about the ransom theory by now. We're way past the Frontier region—there aren't any tribes living out here. The only explanation I can think of is that the guy's completely insane. Who except a lunatic would fly into this kind of place?"

"Well, I know that only an incredibly skilled pilot could," Barnard shot back. "I'm not great at geography, but I know these are supposed to be the highest mountains in the world, and if that's true, it takes some serious flying skills to cross them."

"And it's also God's will," Miss Brinklow added unexpectedly.

Conway didn't offer an opinion. God's will or human insanity—he figured you could pick either one if you wanted a good enough explanation for most things. Or alternatively (and he thought about this as he looked at their neat little cabin against the backdrop of such wild scenery), maybe it was human will and God's insanity. It must be nice to be completely sure which way to look at it.

As Conway watched and thought, something strange happened to the scene before them. The light turned bluish across the whole mountain, with the lower slopes darkening to purple. Something deeper than his usual detachment stirred in him—not quite excitement, definitely not fear, but a sharp sense of anticipation. "You're right, Barnard," he said. "This whole thing is getting more and more extraordinary."

"Extraordinary or not, I'm not about to thank anyone for it," Mallinson insisted. "We didn't ask to be brought here, and who knows what we'll do when we get there—wherever 'there' is. And I don't care if he's some amazing stunt pilot. Even if he is, he can still be completely crazy. I once heard about a pilot who went insane mid-flight. This guy must have been crazy from the start. That's what I think, Conway."

Conway stayed quiet. He was tired of having to shout over the engine noise, and anyway, there wasn't much point in arguing about possibilities. But when Mallinson pressed him for an opinion, he said: "Well, if he's crazy, he's very organized about it. Don't forget that planned fuel stop, and remember this was the only plane that could fly this high."

"That doesn't prove he isn't crazy. He could have been crazy enough to plan everything."

"Yes, that's possible."

"Well, then, we need to decide what we're going to do. What happens when he lands? If he doesn't crash and kill us all, that is. What are we going to do? Run up and congratulate him on his amazing flying skills, I suppose?"

"Not on your life," answered Barnard. "I'll let you do all the running up."

Again Conway didn't want to keep arguing, especially since the American, with his level-headed jokes, seemed perfectly capable of handling the situation. Already Conway found himself thinking that their little group could have been much worse. Only Mallinson was getting really difficult, and that might partly be because of the high altitude. The thin air affected different people in different ways; Conway himself felt a mix of mental clarity and physical laziness that wasn't actually unpleasant. In fact, he found himself taking little breaths of the clear, cold air with a kind of satisfaction. The whole situation was awful, of course, but he couldn't help being fascinated by something that was moving forward so purposefully and with such captivating mystery.

He also felt a surge of appreciation as he stared at that magnificent mountain view—glad that places like this still existed on Earth: distant, unreachable, not yet touched by humans. The icy wall of the Karakorams looked more striking than ever against the northern sky, which had turned grey and threatening. The peaks had an icy gleam; completely majestic and remote, they seemed more dignified for not even having names. Being just a few thousand feet shorter than the most famous peaks might save them forever from climbing expeditions; they weren't quite tempting enough for record-breakers. Conway was the opposite of that type; he thought there was something kind of tacky about the Western obsession with being the biggest and the best. He preferred "pretty high" to "highest" and found the idea of always pushing for extremes kind of boring. He didn't really care for excessive striving and wasn't interested in mere achievements.

While he was still looking at the scene, twilight fell, filling the valleys with rich, dark shadows that spread upward like spilled ink. Then the whole mountain range, much closer now, burst into fresh brilliance; a full moon rose, touching each peak one after another like some heavenly lamplighter, until the whole horizon glittered against a deep blue-black sky. The air got colder and a wind picked up, tossing the plane around uncomfortably. These new discomforts lowered everyone's spirits; they hadn't expected the flight to continue after dark, and now their only hope was that they'd run out of fuel. That had to happen soon, though. Mallinson started arguing about it, and Conway, though he wasn't really sure, estimated they might have flown up to a thousand miles, most of which they must have covered by now. "Well, where would that put us?" Mallinson asked miserably.

"It's hard to be exact, but probably somewhere in Tibet. If these are the Karakorams, Tibet lies beyond them. By the way, one of those peaks must be K2, which is considered the second highest mountain in the world."

"Right after Everest," commented Barnard. "Man, this is some view."

"And from a climber's perspective, much harder than Everest. Even the Duke of Abruzzi gave up on it, said it was completely impossible to climb."

"Oh, God!" muttered Mallinson irritably, but Barnard laughed. "I guess you're our official tour guide on this trip, Conway. And I'll tell you what—if I just had a flask of coffee with brandy in it, I wouldn't care if we were in Tibet or Tennessee."

"But what are we going to DO about it?" Mallinson pressed again. "Why are we here? What's the point of all this? I don't see how you can joke about it."

"Well, it's better than getting all worked up about it, kid. Besides, if the guy's crazy like you think, maybe there isn't any point."

"He must be crazy. I can't think of any other explanation. Can you, Conway?"

Conway shook his head.

Miss Brinklow turned around, like someone during a break at the theater. "Since you haven't asked my opinion, maybe I shouldn't give it," she started, in a high, prim voice, "but I'd like to say that I agree with Mr. Mallinson. I'm sure the poor man can't be right in his head. The pilot, I mean, of course. There would be no excuse for him if he weren't mad." She added, shouting over the noise: "And do you know, this is my first time flying! My very first! Nothing would ever make me do it before, even though a friend tried her hardest to get me to fly from

London to Paris."

"And now you're flying from India to Tibet instead," said Barnard. "That's how life works."

Then suddenly they were all jolted awake by the plane lurching violently. Conway's head hit the window, stunning him for a moment; another lurch sent him stumbling between the rows of seats. It was much colder. The first thing he did, automatically, was check his watch; it showed 1:30 AM—he must have been asleep for quite a while. His ears were filled with a loud flapping sound, which he first thought he was imagining until he realized the engine had been turned off and the plane was fighting against a strong wind. He looked out the window and could see the ground quite close—a vague, snail-grey surface rushing past underneath. "He's going to land!" Mallinson shouted; and Barnard, who had also been thrown from his seat, responded dryly: "If he's lucky." Miss Brinklow, who seemed the least bothered by all the commotion, was calmly adjusting her hat as if they were about to land at a regular airport.

Soon the plane touched ground. But it was a rough landing this time—"Oh God, really bad, really bad!" Mallinson groaned as he held onto his seat during ten seconds of crashing and swaying. They heard something strain and snap, and one of the tires exploded. "That's done it," he added in a tone of total despair. "A broken tail-skid—we're stuck here now, that's for sure."

Conway, who never talked much during emergencies, stretched his stiff legs and felt his head where it had hit the window. Just a bruise—nothing serious. He knew he should do something to help the others. But he was the last of the four to stand up when the plane finally stopped moving. "Careful," he called out as Mallinson yanked open the cabin door and got ready to jump down to the ground. In the strange quiet, the young man's answer came back: "No need to be careful—this looks like the end of the world—there's not another soul around."

A moment later, shivering in the cold, they all realized he was right. With no sound in their ears except the fierce gusts of wind and the crunch of their own footsteps, they felt at the mercy of something grim and terribly lonely—a mood that seemed to fill both the earth and air. The moon had disappeared behind clouds, and starlight revealed an enormous emptiness that seemed to heave with wind. Without even thinking about it, you could tell this bleak world was high in the mountains, and that the mountains rising from it were mountains on top of mountains. A range of them gleamed on the far horizon like a row of sharp teeth.

Mallinson, full of nervous energy, was already heading for the cockpit. "I'm not scared of this guy on the ground, whoever he is," he called out. "I'm going to confront him right now..."

The others watched, frozen by the sight of such determination, though also worried. Conway jumped after him, but too late to stop him. After a few seconds, though, the young man climbed back down, grabbing Conway's arm and speaking in rough, sobered bursts: "Conway... it's weird... I think the guy's sick or dead or something... I can't get him to say anything. Come look... I got his gun, anyway."

"Better give it to me," said Conway, and though he was still a bit dazed from hitting his head, he prepared himself for action. Of all the times and places and situations on Earth, this seemed to combine the absolute worst discomforts. He pulled himself up to where he could see, not very well, into the enclosed cockpit. There was a strong smell of fuel, so he didn't risk lighting a match. He could just make out the pilot, slumped forward with his head sprawled over the controls. He shook him, took off his helmet, and loosened the clothes around his neck. A moment later he turned to report: "Yes, something's wrong with him. We need to get him out." But an observer might have noticed that something had changed about Conway too. His voice was sharper, more decisive; he no longer seemed caught between different possibilities. The time, the place, the cold, his tiredness—they all mattered less now; there was a job that had to be done, and the more practical part of him took over to do it.

With Barnard and Mallinson helping, they got the pilot out of his seat and lowered him to the ground. He was unconscious but not dead. Conway didn't have any special medical training, but like most people who had lived in remote places, he was familiar with various kinds of illness. "Probably a heart attack brought on by the high altitude," he said, examining the mysterious man. "We can't do much for him out here—there's no shelter from this terrible wind. We should get him inside the cabin, and ourselves too. We have no idea where we are, and it's hopeless to try going anywhere until daylight."

Everyone accepted his diagnosis and suggestion without argument. Even Mallinson agreed. They carried the man into the cabin and laid him in the aisle between the seats. The inside wasn't any warmer than outside, but at least it blocked the wind. And it was the wind, as time passed, that became everyone's main concern—the central feature of this whole gloomy night scene. It wasn't an ordinary wind. It wasn't just a strong wind or a cold wind. It was like some kind of fury that lived all around them, a master stamping and raging over its own territory. It rocked the heavy plane and shook it viciously, and when Conway looked through the windows, it seemed like the same wind was tearing sparkles of light from the stars.

The pilot lay motionless while Conway did his best to examine him in the dim light and cramped space. It didn't reveal much. "His heart's weak," he said, and then Miss Brinklow, after digging in her handbag, created a small surprise. "I wonder if this might help the poor man," she offered condescendingly. "I never drink it myself, but I always carry it in case of emergencies. And this is sort of an emergency, isn't it?"

"I'd say it definitely is," Conway replied grimly. He unscrewed the bottle, smelled it, and poured some of the brandy into the man's mouth. "Just what he needs. Thanks." After a while, they could see the slightest movement of his eyelids in the match light. Mallinson suddenly got hysterical. "I can't help it," he cried, laughing wildly. "We all look so ridiculous striking matches over a dying man... And he's not much to look at, is he? Chinese, I'd guess, if he's anything."

"Probably," Conway's voice was level and a bit stern. "But he's not dead yet. With some luck we might bring him around."

"Luck? It'll be his luck, not ours."

"Don't be too sure. And be quiet for now, anyway."

There was still enough of the schoolboy in Mallinson to make him obey a sharp command from someone older, though he clearly wasn't handling things well. Conway felt sorry for him but was more focused on the immediate problem of the pilot, since he was the only one who might be able to explain their situation. Conway didn't want to keep speculating about it; they'd done enough of that during the flight. He was worried now beyond just being curious, because he realized their whole situation had stopped being excitingly dangerous and was becoming a test of survival that might end in disaster. Throughout that wind-tortured night, he faced facts honestly, though he didn't bother sharing them with the others. He guessed they had flown far beyond the western edge of the Himalayas toward the less-known peaks of the Kunlun Mountains. If that was true, they would now be in the highest and most inhospitable part of Earth's surface—the Tibetan plateau, two miles high even in its lowest valleys, a vast, uninhabited, and mostly unexplored region of windswept highlands. They were stranded somewhere in that desolate country, worse off than on most desert islands.

Then suddenly, as if to answer his thoughts by making them even more mysterious, something amazing happened. The moon, which he'd thought was hidden by clouds, came over the edge of a dark mountain and, while still not showing itself directly, lit up the darkness ahead. Conway could see the outline of a long valley, with rounded, sad-looking hills on either side, not very high from where they rose, and black against the deep electric blue of the night sky. But it was the head of the valley that caught his eyes irresistibly, for there, soaring into the gap and magnificent in the full moonlight, stood what he thought must be the most beautiful mountain on Earth. It was an almost perfect cone of snow, so simple in shape it looked like a child had drawn it, and impossible to judge its size, height, or distance. It was so radiant, so perfectly balanced, that for a moment he wondered if it was even real. Then, while he watched, a tiny puff of cloud appeared at the edge of the pyramid, bringing the vision to life just before the faint rumble of an avalanche confirmed it.

He felt like waking the others to share the sight but decided it probably wouldn't help calm them down. And from a practical view, such pure, untouched beauty only emphasized how isolated and dangerous their situation was. There was a good chance the nearest human settlement was hundreds of miles away. They had no food; they only had one gun; the plane was damaged and almost out of fuel, even if any of them knew how to fly it. They had no clothes suitable for the terrible cold and wind; Mallinson's driving coat and his own heavy coat weren't nearly enough, and even Miss Brinklow, bundled up like she was heading to the North Pole (which had seemed ridiculous when he first saw her), couldn't be comfortable. They were all affected by the high altitude too, except for him. Even Barnard had sunk into depression under the strain. Mallinson was muttering to himself; it was clear what would happen to him if these hardships continued much longer.

The pilot started speaking in bursts. The four passengers leaned close, listening hard to sounds that made no sense except to Conway, who occasionally answered. After some time, the man grew weaker, had more trouble talking, and finally died. That was around mid-morning.

Conway turned to his companions. "I'm sorry to say he didn't tell me much—not much compared to what we'd like to know. Just that we're in Tibet, which is obvious. He didn't give any clear explanation of why he brought us here, but he seemed to know the area. He spoke a kind of Chinese I don't understand very well, but I think he said something about a monastery nearby—along the valley, I think—where we could get food and shelter. He called it Shangri-La. 'La' means mountain pass in Tibetan. He was really insistent that we should go there."

"Which doesn't seem like any reason why we should," said Mallinson. "After all, he was probably crazy, wasn't he?"

"You know as much about that as I do. But if we don't go to this place, where else can we go?"

"Anywhere, I don't care. All I know is that this Shangri-La, if it's in that direction, must be even further from civilization. I'd feel better if we were getting closer to it, not further away. Come on, Conway, aren't you going to get us back?"

Conway answered patiently: "I don't think you really understand the situation, Mallinson. We're in a part of the world that nobody knows much about, except that it's difficult and dangerous even for a properly equipped expedition. When you consider that hundreds of miles of this kind of country probably surround us on all sides, walking back to Peshawar doesn't seem very realistic."

"I don't think I could possibly do it," said Miss Brinklow seriously.

Barnard nodded. "Looks like we're pretty lucky, then, if this monastery is just around the corner."

"Relatively lucky, maybe," agreed Conway. "After all, we have no food, and as you can see, this isn't exactly a country where it's easy to find any. In a few hours we'll all be starving. And tonight, if we stayed here, we'd have to face the wind and cold again. It's not a great situation. Our only chance seems to be finding other human beings, and where else should we look for them except where we've been told they exist?"

"And what if it's a trap?" asked Mallinson, but Barnard had an answer. "A nice warm trap with some food in it would suit me just fine right now."

They laughed, except Mallinson, who looked stressed and on edge. Finally Conway continued: "So I take it we're all more or less agreed? There's an obvious path along the valley—it doesn't look too steep, though we'll have to take it slowly. In any case, we can't do anything here—we couldn't even bury this man without explosives. Besides, the monastery people might be able to give us porters for the journey back. We'll need them. I suggest we start now, so if we don't find the place by late afternoon, we'll have time to come back for another night in the cabin."

"And supposing we do find it?" pressed Mallinson, still resistant. "Do we have any guarantee we won't be murdered?"

"None at all. But I think it's a smaller, and maybe also a preferable risk to starving or freezing to death." He added, feeling that such cold logic might not be the best approach: "Actually, murder is about the last thing you'd expect in a Buddhist monastery. It would be even less likely than being killed in an English cathedral."

"Like Thomas Becket," said Miss Brinklow, nodding vigorously in agreement but completely ruining his point. Mallinson shrugged his shoulders and answered irritably: "Fine then, let's head off to Shangri-La. Whatever and wherever it is, we'll try it. But let's hope it's not halfway up that mountain."

The comment made them all look at the glittering snow cone toward which the valley pointed. It looked absolutely magnificent in the full daylight; and then their stares turned to shock, because they could see, far away and coming down the slope toward them, the figures of people. "Providence!" whispered Miss Brinklow.

CHAPTER 3

Part of Conway was always watching things unfold, even when the rest of him was in the middle of the action. Now, as they waited for the strangers to come closer, he refused to get worked up about all the different things that might or might not happen. This wasn't because he was brave, or cool under pressure, or supremely confident in his ability to make split-second decisions. If anything, it was a kind of laziness—he just didn't want to interrupt his role as an observer of whatever was happening.

As the figures moved down the valley, they turned out to be a group of twelve or more people, carrying what looked like a covered chair. In it sat someone wearing blue robes. Conway had no idea where they were all going, but it definitely seemed like luck—or "providence" as Miss Brinklow had said—that such a group would happen to be passing by right then. When they got close enough to call out to, he walked forward to meet them, though not too quickly, because he knew that in Asia, people liked to take their time with greetings and follow certain customs. He stopped a few yards away and bowed politely. To his surprise, the person in blue robes stepped down from the chair, came forward with dignified slowness, and held out his hand. Conway shook it and found himself looking at an elderly Chinese man with grey hair and a clean-shaven face, who looked somehow elegant even here, wearing an embroidered silk robe. The man seemed to be studying Conway just as carefully. Then, in perfect—almost too perfect—English, he said: "I am from the lamasery of Shangri-La."

Conway bowed again, and after a proper pause, started explaining briefly how he and his three companions had ended up in such a remote part of the world. When he finished, the Chinese man made a gesture of understanding. "That is quite remarkable," he said, looking thoughtfully at the damaged plane. Then he added: "My name is Chang, if you would be so kind as to introduce me to your friends."

Conway managed to hide his amusement with a polite smile. He was rather intrigued by this latest surprise—a Chinese man who spoke perfect English and acted like he was at a London social club, here in the middle of Tibet. He turned to the others, who had caught up by now and were staring at the encounter with various levels of amazement. "Miss Brinklow... Mr. Barnard, who's American... Mr. Mallinson... and I'm Conway. We're all very glad to see you, though this meeting is almost as puzzling as how we got here in the first place. Actually, we were just about to try finding our way to your lamasery, so this is doubly fortunate. If you could just give us directions—"

"There's no need for that. I would be delighted to guide you myself."

"Oh, I couldn't possibly put you to so much trouble. It's very kind of you, but if it's not far—"

"It is not far, but it is not easy either. I would consider it an honor to accompany you and your friends."

"But really—"

"I must insist."

Conway thought that this back-and-forth, given where they were and what was happening, was starting to get a bit ridiculous. "Very well," he said. "We're all very grateful."

Mallinson, who had been glumly enduring all these polite exchanges, now cut in with the sharp tone of someone used to giving orders. "We won't be staying long," he announced bluntly. "We'll pay for whatever we need, and we'd like to hire some of your men to help us on our journey back. We want to return to civilization as soon as possible."

"And are you so very sure that you are away from it?"

This smooth response only made Mallinson more irritated. "I'm quite sure I'm far from where I want to be, and so are we all. We'll be grateful for temporary shelter, but we'll be even more grateful if you'll help us get back. How long do you think the journey to India will take?"

"I really couldn't say."

"Well, I hope we're not going to have any trouble about it. I've dealt with local porters before, and we expect you to use your influence to get us a fair deal."

Conway felt this was all unnecessarily aggressive, and he was about to step in when Chang replied, still incredibly dignified: "I can only assure you, Mr. Mallinson, that you will be treated with honor and that ultimately you will have no regrets."

"Ultimately?" Mallinson jumped on the word, but fortunately things got easier to handle when wine and fruit appeared, brought out by the other members of the group—sturdy Tibetans wearing sheepskin clothes, fur hats, and boots made from yak hide. The wine tasted pleasant, similar to a good German white wine, and the fruit included mangoes that were perfectly ripe and incredibly delicious after so many hours without food. Mallinson ate and drank without asking questions, but Conway, relieved of immediate worries and not wanting to worry about distant ones, wondered how they managed to grow mangoes at such a high altitude.

He was also fascinated by the mountain rising beyond the valley. It was an incredible peak by any standard, and he was surprised that no explorer had ever written about it in one of those books that everyone seems to write after traveling in Tibet. In his mind, he started climbing it, planning a route up ridges and through passes until Mallinson's exclamation brought him back to earth. He looked around and saw that Chang had been studying him closely. "You were looking at the mountain, Mr. Conway?" he asked.

"Yes. It's magnificent. Does it have a name?"

"It is called Karakal."

"I don't think I've ever heard of it. Is it very high?"

"Over twenty-eight thousand feet."

"Really? I didn't know there was anything that big outside the Himalayas. Has it been properly measured? Who did the measurements?"

"Who would you expect, my dear sir? Is there anything that makes monasticism incompatible with trigonometry?"

Conway appreciated the clever phrase and replied: "Oh, not at all —not at all." Then he laughed politely. He thought it wasn't the best joke, but maybe worth playing along with. Soon after that, they began their journey to Shangri-La.

They climbed all morning, slowly and on gentle slopes, but at this altitude even that was hard work, and no one had energy for talking. Chang traveled comfortably in his chair, which might have seemed ungentlemanly if it hadn't been ridiculous to picture Miss Brinklow in such a royal setup. Conway, who was less affected by the thin air than the others, tried to catch bits of conversation from the chair-bearers. He knew a tiny bit of Tibetan, just enough to understand that the men were happy to be heading back to the lamasery. He couldn't have continued talking to Chang even if he'd wanted to, since the latter, with his eyes closed and face half-hidden behind curtains, seemed to have mastered the art of taking perfectly timed naps.

Meanwhile the sun was warm; they weren't as hungry or thirsty anymore, though they weren't exactly satisfied; and the air, clean like it came from another planet, became more precious with every breath. They had to breathe consciously and deliberately, which felt weird at first but eventually led to an almost magical feeling of peace. Your whole body fell into a single rhythm of breathing, walking, and thinking; your lungs, no longer working automatically without you noticing, had to work in harmony with your mind and body. Conway, who had both a mystical side and a skeptical one working strangely well together, found himself pleasantly puzzled by the sensation. He occasionally said something encouraging to Mallinson, but the young man was struggling with the climb. Barnard was wheezing like he had asthma, while Miss Brinklow was fighting some kind of battle with her breathing that for some reason she tried to hide. "We're almost at the top," Conway said encouragingly.

"I once ran for a train and felt just like this," she answered.

And some people, Conway thought to himself, think apple juice is just like champagne. It's all about what you're used to.

He was surprised to find that beyond his confusion about the situation, he didn't have many worries, at least not for himself. There are moments in life when you open your mind to new experiences just like you might open your wallet wider if an evening's entertainment turns out to be more expensive than expected but also more interesting than you thought it would be. Conway, on that breathless morning in view of Karakal, had exactly that kind of willing, relieved, but not over-excited response to the offer of a new adventure. After ten years in various parts of Asia, he'd developed pretty particular tastes about places and events, and he had to admit this one promised to be unusual.

About two miles along the valley, the climb got steeper, but by then the sun had disappeared behind clouds and a silvery mist blocked their view. Thunder and avalanches echoed from the snow-fields above; the air got chilly, and then, with the sudden changes typical of mountain regions, turned bitterly cold. A blast of wind and sleet hit them, soaking everyone and making everything much worse. Even Conway felt for a moment that they couldn't possibly go much further. But soon after that, it seemed they'd reached the top of the ridge, because the chair-bearers stopped to adjust their load. Barnard and Mallinson were both suffering badly, which caused more delays, but the Tibetans were clearly eager to keep moving and made signs that the rest of the journey would be easier.

After these promises, it was disappointing to see them getting out ropes. "Are they planning to hang us already?" Barnard managed to joke weakly, but the guides soon showed that their less sinister plan was just to tie everyone together like normal mountain climbers. When they saw that Conway knew about rope techniques, they became much more respectful and let him arrange the group his own way. He put himself next to Mallinson, with Tibetans in front and behind, and with Barnard, Miss Brinklow, and more Tibetans further back. He quickly noticed that while Chang was sleeping, the men were happy to let him take charge. He felt a familiar sense of leadership rising; if things got difficult, he would give what he knew was his to give —confidence and control. He had been a first-class mountain climber in his time and was probably still pretty good. "You've got to look after Barnard," he told Miss Brinklow, half-joking but half-serious; and she answered, with the boldness of an eagle: "I'll do my best, but you know, I've never been roped up before."

The next part, though exciting at times, wasn't as exhausting as he'd expected, and it was actually a relief after the lung-bursting climb. The path was cut into the side of a rock wall that disappeared into the mist above them. Maybe it was lucky that the mist also hid the drop on the other side, though Conway, who was good at judging heights, would have liked to see where they were. The path was barely two feet wide in places, and the way the bearers managed Chang's chair through these spots impressed Conway almost as much as the nerves of Chang himself, who could somehow sleep through it all. The Tibetans were reliable enough, but they seemed happier when the path widened and started going slightly downhill. Then they began singing among themselves—wild, beautiful tunes that Conway could imagine being turned into an exotic ballet. The rain stopped and the air grew warmer. "Well, we definitely couldn't have found our way here by ourselves," said Conway, trying to be cheerful, but Mallinson didn't find that very comforting. He was actually terrified, and now that the worst was over, he was in more danger of showing it. "Would we want to?" he shot back bitterly.

The path continued downhill more steeply, and at one point Conway found some edelweiss, the first welcome sign of more hospitable territory. But when he mentioned this, it only made Mallinson more upset. "Good God, Conway, do you think you're hiking in the Alps? What kind of nightmare place are we heading to? That's what I'd like to know! And what's our plan when we get there? What are we going to do?"

Conway said quietly: "If you'd had all the experiences I've had, you'd know that sometimes in life the most comfortable thing is to do nothing at all. Things happen to you and you just let them happen. The War was kind of like that. You're lucky if, like now, there's at least something new about the unpleasantness."

"You're too philosophical for me. That wasn't how you acted during the trouble in Baskul."

"Of course not, because then there was a chance I could change things by what I did. But now, at least for the moment, there's no such chance. We're here because we're here, if you want a reason. I usually find that a comforting thought."

"Do you realize what an awful job it'll be to get back the way we came? We've been inching along the face of a straight-up mountain for the last hour—I've been paying attention."

"So have I."

"Have you?" Mallinson coughed nervously. "I know I'm being annoying, but I can't help it. I'm suspicious about all this. I feel like we're doing exactly what these people want us to. They're getting us trapped."

"Even if they are, the only other choice was to stay out there and die."

"I know that's logical, but it doesn't help. I don't find it as easy as you do to just accept what's happening. I can't forget that two days ago we were in the Consulate at Baskul. Everything that's happened since then is overwhelming. I'm sorry. I'm not thinking straight. It makes me realize how lucky I was to miss the War—I probably would have gotten hysterical about everything. The whole world seems to have gone completely crazy around me. I must be pretty crazy myself to be talking to you like this."

Conway shook his head. "My dear boy, not at all. You're twenty-four years old, and you're about two and a half miles up in the air—those are reason enough for anything you might be feeling right now. I think you've handled an incredibly difficult situation amazingly well—better than I would have at your age."

"But don't you feel how crazy it all is?" Mallinson pressed. "The way we flew over those mountains, and that awful waiting in the wind, and the pilot dying, and then meeting these people—doesn't it all seem like a nightmare when you think about it?"

"It does, of course."

"Then I wish I knew how you manage to stay so calm about everything."

"Do you really want to know? I'll tell you, though you might think I'm being cynical. It's because so much else I've seen seems like a nightmare too. This isn't the only crazy part of the world, Mallinson. If you think about Baskul, remember just before we left how the revolutionaries were torturing people to get information? And remember the last message that came through before we lost contact? It was from a Manchester clothing company asking if we knew anyone in Baskul who might want to buy corsets! Isn't that crazy enough for you? Trust me, the worst that's happened is we've traded one kind of madness for another. And as for the War, if you'd been in it you'd have done what I did—learned how to be scared while keeping a straight face."

They were still talking when a short but steep climb left them breathless, bringing back all their earlier exhaustion. But soon the ground leveled out, and they stepped out of the mist into clear, sunny air. Ahead, just a short distance away, stood the lamasery of Shangri-La.

To Conway, seeing it first, it might have been a vision floating out of that lonely rhythm his oxygen-starved brain had fallen into. It was, without a doubt, an amazing and almost unbelievable sight. A collection of colorful buildings clung to the mountainside, not with the heavy determination of a German castle, but with the delicate chance beauty of flower petals caught on a cliff. It was stunning and perfect. Your eye was drawn upward from the soft blue roofs to the grey rock fortress above, as massive as the great mountains of Switzerland. Beyond that, in a dazzling triangle, rose the snow-covered slopes of Karakal. This might well be, Conway thought, the most awe-inspiring mountain view in the world, and he imagined the immense pressure of snow and ice pushing against the rock that acted as a giant retaining wall. Someday, perhaps, the whole mountain would split, and half of Karakal's icy magnificence would come crashing into the valley. He wondered if the tiny chance of that happening, combined with how terrifying it would be, might actually make living here more exciting.

The view down was just as enticing, because the mountain wall dropped almost straight down into a gap that must have been created by some ancient earthquake. The valley floor, hazy in the distance, welcomed the eye with its greenness. Protected from winds and watched over rather than dominated by the lamasery, it looked to Conway like a wonderfully blessed place, though if anyone lived there they must be completely cut off by the tall, absolutely unclimbable mountain ranges on the other side. The only way in or out seemed to be through the lamasery itself. As he looked, Conway felt a slight tightening of worry; maybe Mallinson's concerns weren't completely crazy. But the feeling only lasted a moment before merging into a deeper sensation, part spiritual and part visual, of having finally reached somewhere that was an ending, a destination.

He never quite remembered exactly how they got to the lamasery, or what formal welcome they received when they were untied from the ropes and shown inside. The thin air made everything feel dreamlike, matching the porcelain-blue of the sky; with every breath and every look around, he felt a deep, calming peace that made him immune to Mallinson's anxiety, Barnard's jokes, and Miss Brinklow's prim way of acting like a proper lady prepared for the worst. He vaguely remembered being surprised to find the inside spacious, well heated, and very clean; but there wasn't time to notice much more than that, because Chang had left his covered chair and was already leading them through various rooms. He was quite friendly now. "I must apologize," he said, "for keeping to myself during the journey, but the truth is, trips like that don't agree with me, and I have to be careful. I hope you weren't too tired?"

"We managed," replied Conway with a slight smile.

"Excellent. And now, if you'll come with me, I'll show you to your rooms. You'd probably like baths. Our accommodations are simple, but I hope they'll do."

At this point Barnard, who was still having trouble breathing, let out a wheezy laugh. "Well," he gasped, "I can't say I like your climate yet—the air seems to stick in my chest—but you've certainly got an amazing view from your front windows. Do we all have to line up for the bathroom, or is this like an American hotel?"

"I think you'll find everything quite satisfactory, Mr. Barnard."

Miss Brinklow nodded stiffly. "I should certainly hope so."

"And afterward," continued Chang, "I would be greatly honored if you would all join me for dinner."

Conway replied politely. Only Mallinson hadn't shown any reaction to these unexpected comforts. Like Barnard, he'd been struggling with the altitude, but now, with effort, he found breath to exclaim: "And afterward, if you don't mind, we'll make our plans for getting out of here. The sooner the better, as far as I'm concerned."

The contrast between the amazing beauty they'd just seen and Mallinson's determination to leave hung in the air like the strange, thin atmosphere around them. Conway found himself wondering, not for the first time since their arrival, if perhaps there was something more to Shangri-La than any of them yet understood.

CHAPTER 4

"So you see," Chang was saying, "we're not as primitive as you might have expected..."

Conway, relaxing later that evening, couldn't argue with that. He was enjoying that perfect mix of physical comfort and mental alertness that seemed to him the truest mark of civilization. So far, Shangri-La had offered everything he could have wanted —definitely more than he could have expected. Finding central heating in a Tibetan monastery wasn't maybe so shocking in an age when even Lhasa had telephones, but the way it combined modern Western convenience with Eastern tradition really impressed him. The bathtub, for instance, where he'd just enjoyed a wonderful soak, had been gleaming green porcelain, made (according to the label) in Akron, Ohio. But the attendant had taken care of him in traditional Chinese style, cleaning his ears and nostrils, and even gently wiping under his lower eyelids with a silk swab. He wondered if his three companions were getting similar treatment.

Conway had lived in China for almost ten years, not just in the big cities, and he considered it the happiest time of his life. He liked Chinese people and felt comfortable with their ways. He especially loved Chinese cooking, with its subtle flavors, so his first meal at Shangri-La had felt wonderfully familiar. He suspected they might have added some herb or medicine to help with breathing, because not only did he feel better, but he could see his fellow guests were breathing more easily too. He noticed that Chang ate only a small portion of green salad and drank no wine. "You'll excuse me," he had explained at the start, "but I have to follow a very strict diet—I must take care of myself."

He'd given this reason before, and Conway wondered what kind of health problem he had. Looking at him more closely now, Conway found it hard to guess his age; his small, somehow undefined features and his smooth, clay-like skin made him look either like a young man who had aged early or an old man who had aged incredibly well. He wasn't unattractive; there was a certain formal politeness about him that hung in the air like a very faint perfume—you wouldn't notice it until you stopped thinking about it. In his embroidered blue silk robe, with the traditional side-split skirt and tight-ankled trousers, all colored like watercolor skies, he had a cool, metallic charm that Conway found pleasant, though he knew not everyone would agree.

The whole atmosphere was more Chinese than specifically Tibetan, which made Conway feel at home, though he knew his companions wouldn't share that feeling. The room pleased him too; it was perfectly proportioned and decorated simply with tapestries and a few beautiful lacquered pieces. Light came from paper lanterns that hung motionless in the still air. He felt peaceful in both body and mind, and his thoughts about possible medicine in the food didn't worry him much. Whatever it was, if it existed at all, it had helped Barnard's breathing problems and Mallinson's aggression; both had eaten well, focusing on their food rather than conversation. Conway had been quite hungry too, and he was glad that good manners meant taking things slowly here. He never liked rushing through enjoyable situations, so this approach suited him perfectly. It wasn't until he'd started smoking a cigarette that he gently began asking questions. "You seem to have a very fortunate community here," he remarked to Chang, "and you're very welcoming to strangers. Though I imagine you don't get many visitors."

"Very rarely indeed," replied Chang with measured dignity. "This is not a well-traveled part of the world."

Conway smiled at that understatement. "You put it mildly. When we were arriving, this looked like the most isolated place I'd ever seen. A separate culture could develop here without any influence from the outside world."

"Influence, would you say?"

"I'm thinking of things like jazz bands, movie theaters, neon signs, and so on. Your plumbing is quite rightly as modern as you can get it—that's the one real gift the West can offer the East, in my opinion. I often think the Romans were lucky—their civilization got as far as hot baths without discovering the dangerous knowledge of machines."

Conway paused. He'd been talking smoothly and naturally, but with a purpose—he was good at creating and controlling atmosphere through conversation. He was skilled at that sort of thing. Only respect for their host's extremely polite manner kept him from asking more direct questions.

Miss Brinklow, however, had no such hesitation. "Please," she said, though she didn't sound very humble about it, "tell us about the monastery."

Chang raised his eyebrows very slightly, showing gentle

disapproval of such directness. "It will give me the greatest pleasure, madam, as far as I am able. What exactly would you like to know?"

"First, how many of you are there here, and what nationalities are you?" It was clear her organized mind was working just as efficiently as it had at the mission house in Baskul.

Chang replied: "Those of us who are full lamas number about fifty, and there are a few others, like myself, who haven't yet reached complete initiation. We hope to do so in due course. Until then we are half-lamas—you might say novices. As for our backgrounds, we have people from many nations among us, though naturally Tibetans and Chinese make up the majority."

Miss Brinklow never hesitated to jump to conclusions—even wrong ones. "I see. So it's really a native monastery, then. Is your head lama Tibetan or Chinese?"

"No."

"Are there any English people?"

"Several."

"Well, that's very surprising." Miss Brinklow paused only to catch her breath before continuing: "And now, tell me what you all believe in."

Conway leaned back, amused and curious. He always enjoyed

watching different types of minds clash, and Miss Brinklow's Girl Scout directness applied to Buddhist philosophy promised to be entertaining. But he didn't want their host to feel attacked. "That's quite a big question," he said diplomatically.

But Miss Brinklow wasn't in a diplomatic mood. The wine, which had made the others more relaxed, seemed to have made her more energetic. "Of course," she said with a gesture of generosity, "I believe in the true religion, but I'm open-minded enough to accept that other people—foreigners, I mean—often honestly believe in their views. And naturally in a monastery I wouldn't expect people to agree with me."

Chang gave her a formal bow. "But why not, madam?" he replied in his precise and cultured English. "Must we assume that because one religion is true, all others must be false?"

"Well, of course, that's rather obvious, isn't it?"

Conway stepped in again. "Really, I think we'd better not argue. But Miss Brinklow shares my curiosity about the purpose of this unique place."

Chang answered slowly, almost whispering: "If I had to put it very simply, my dear sir, I would say that our main belief is in moderation. We teach the value of avoiding excess of all kinds —even including, if you'll pardon the paradox, excess of virtue itself. In the valley you've seen, where several thousand people live under our order's guidance, we've found that this principle leads to considerable happiness. We rule with moderate strictness, and in return we accept moderate obedience. And I think I can say that our people are moderately sober, moderately well-behaved, and moderately honest."

Conway smiled. He thought it was well expressed, and it appealed to his own nature. "I think I understand. And I suppose the men who met us this morning were from your valley people?"

"Yes. I hope you had no complaints about them during the journey?"

"Oh no, none at all. I'm glad they were more than moderately sure-footed, anyway. You were careful, by the way, to say that the rule of moderation applied to them—should I take it that it doesn't apply to your priesthood?"

But Chang could only shake his head. "I'm sorry, sir, but you've touched on something I cannot discuss. I can only say that our community has various beliefs and practices, but most of us are moderately unorthodox about them. I deeply regret that I cannot say more at the moment."

"Please don't apologize. You leave me with the most interesting speculations." Something in his own voice, along with his physical sensations, made Conway again suspect they'd been given some mild drug. Mallinson seemed similarly affected, though he used this chance to say: "All this has been very interesting, but I really think it's time we started planning how to get away. We need to return to India as soon as possible. How many porters can you provide us with?"

The question, so practical and direct, broke through the polite atmosphere and found no solid ground beneath. Only after a long pause came Chang's reply: "Unfortunately, Mr. Mallinson, I am not the person to ask about that. But in any case, I don't think it could be arranged immediately."

"But something has to be arranged! We all have work to get back to, and our friends and families will be worrying about us—we simply must return. We're grateful for your hospitality, but we can't just hang around here doing nothing. If it's at all possible, we'd like to leave tomorrow. I expect many of your people would volunteer to guide us—we'd make it worth their while, of course."

Mallinson finished nervously, as if he'd hoped for an answer before saying so much, but all he got from Chang was a quiet and almost reproachful: "But all this, you know, is not really my responsibility."

"Isn't it? Well, maybe you can at least help with something. If you could get us a detailed map of the region, that would help. It looks like we'll have a long journey, and that's all the more reason to start soon. You have maps, don't you?"

"Yes, we have many."

"We'll borrow some then, if you don't mind. We can return them later—I assume you must have some contact with the outside world occasionally. And it would be good to send messages ahead too, to reassure our friends. How far away is the nearest telegraph line?"

Chang's wrinkled face seemed to take on a look of infinite patience, but he didn't reply.

Mallinson waited a moment and then continued: "Well, where do you send to when you need something? Something modern, I mean." A hint of fear began to show in his eyes and voice. Suddenly he pushed back his chair and stood up. He was pale and pressed his hand against his forehead. "I'm so tired," he stammered, looking around the room. "I don't feel like any of you are really trying to help. I'm only asking a simple question. Obviously you must know the answer. When you got all these modern bathrooms installed, how did they get here?"

Another silence followed.

"You won't tell me, then? It's part of the mystery of everything else, I suppose. Conway, I must say I think you're being terribly passive—why don't you get to the bottom of this? I'm exhausted for now—but—tomorrow, remember—we must leave tomorrow—it's essential—"

He would have collapsed if Conway hadn't caught him and helped him to a chair. He recovered a bit, but didn't speak.

"Tomorrow he will feel much better," said Chang gently. "The air here is difficult for newcomers at first, but one soon gets used to it."

Conway felt like he was waking from a dream. "Things have been rough for him," he commented mildly. Then, more energetically: "I expect we're all feeling it somewhat—I think we'd better end this discussion and go to bed. Barnard, would you look after Mallinson? And I'm sure you need rest too, Miss Brinklow." Someone must have given a signal, because just then a servant appeared. "Yes, let's all turn in—good night—good night—I'll follow soon." He practically pushed them out of the room, and then, dropping the politeness he'd shown earlier, turned to Chang. Mallinson's criticism had spurred him to action.

"Now, sir," Conway said, "I don't want to keep you long, so I'll get straight to the point. My friend is impatient, but I don't blame him—he's right to want clear answers. We need help arranging our return journey, and we can't do it without assistance from you or others here. Of course I realize leaving tomorrow is impossible, and personally, I might find a short stay quite interesting. But that's not how my companions feel. So if it's true that you can't help us yourself, please put us in touch with someone who can."

The Chinese answered: "You are wiser than your friends, my dear sir, and therefore less impatient. I am glad."

"That's not an answer."

Chang started to laugh—a forced, high-pitched chuckle that Conway recognized as the polite Chinese way of pretending to see a joke when faced with an awkward situation. "I'm sure you have no reason to worry," he said after a pause. "No doubt in time we'll be able to give you all the help you need. There are difficulties, as you can imagine, but if we all approach the problem sensibly, and without rushing—"

"I'm not suggesting rushing. I'm just asking about porters."

"Well, my dear sir, that raises another issue. I very much doubt you'll easily find men willing to make such a journey. They have their homes in the valley, and they don't like leaving them for long, difficult trips outside."

"But they can be convinced to do so, or why and where were they escorting you this morning?"

"This morning? Oh, that was quite different."

"How? Weren't you starting a journey when we happened to meet you?"

There was no response, and eventually Conway continued more quietly: "I see. Then it wasn't a chance meeting. I'd wondered about that all along. So you came there deliberately to meet us. That suggests you must have known we were coming. And the interesting question is: How?"

His words created a moment of tension in the peaceful scene. The lantern light showed Chang's face clearly; it was calm as a statue. Suddenly, with a small gesture, Chang broke the tension; pulling aside a silk tapestry, he revealed a window leading to a balcony. Then, touching Conway's arm, he led him into the cold, crystal-clear air. "You are clever," he said dreamily, "but not entirely correct. For that reason, I would advise you not to worry your friends with these abstract questions. Believe me, neither you nor they are in any danger at Shangri-La."

"But it's not danger we're worried about. It's delay."

"I understand that. And of course there may be some delay—quite unavoidably."

"If it's only for a short time, and genuinely unavoidable, then naturally we'll have to deal with it as best we can."

"How very sensible, for we want nothing more than for you and your companions to enjoy every moment of your stay here."

"That's all very well, and as I said, personally I won't mind too much—it's a new and interesting experience, and anyway, we need some rest."

He was looking up at the gleaming pyramid of Karakal. In the bright moonlight, it seemed so close you might reach up and touch it; it stood crystal-clear against the vast blue beyond.

"Tomorrow," said Chang, "you may find it even more interesting. And as for rest, if you are tired, there are few better places in the world."

Indeed, as Conway kept gazing, he felt an even deeper peace settle over him, as if the view nourished both his mind and eyes. There was barely any wind, unlike the mountain gales that had raged the night before; the whole valley, he realized, was like a sheltered harbor, with Karakal watching over it like a lighthouse. The comparison grew as he thought about it, because there actually was light on the summit, an ice-blue gleam that matched the splendor it reflected. Something made him ask what the name meant, and Chang's answer came like an echo of his own thoughts. "Karakal, in the local dialect, means Blue Moon," said the Chinese.

Conway decided not to tell the others his conclusion that their arrival at Shangri-La had somehow been expected by its inhabitants. He knew he should, and he knew it was important, but when morning came, the knowledge bothered him so little, except theoretically, that he couldn't bring himself to cause more worry for the others. Part of him insisted that something was definitely strange about the place, that Chang's attitude the previous evening had been far from reassuring, and that they were basically prisoners unless and until the authorities chose to help them more. And he clearly had a duty to force them to act. After all, he was a British Government representative; it was outrageous that the members of a Tibetan monastery should refuse any reasonable request...

That would be the normal official view, and part of Conway was both normal and official. No one could better play the strong leader when needed; during those final difficult days before the evacuation, he had acted in a way that (he thought wryly) should earn him nothing less than a knighthood and a spot in a boys' adventure book called "With Conway at Baskul." Taking charge of dozens of civilians including women and children, sheltering them all in a small consulate during a violent revolution led by anti-foreign rebels, and managing to convince the revolutionaries to allow an evacuation by air—it wasn't a bad achievement. Maybe by pulling strings and writing endless reports, he could get something out of it in the next New Year's Honours. At least it had won him Mallinson's complete admiration. Unfortunately the young man must now find him disappointing. It was a shame, but Conway was used to people liking him only because they misunderstood him. He wasn't really one of those determined, square-jawed empire-builders; his performance had been just a short act, repeated occasionally by arrangement with fate and the Foreign Office, for a salary anyone could look up in the government directory.

The truth was, the mystery of Shangri-La and how they'd gotten there was beginning to fascinate him. Besides, he found it hard to feel personally worried. His official job often took him to strange places, and the stranger they were, the less, usually, he got bored; so why complain because accident, instead of orders from London, had brought him to this strangest place of all?

In fact, he was far from complaining. When he woke up in the morning and saw the soft blue sky through his window, he wouldn't have chosen to be anywhere else on Earth—not in Peshawar or Piccadilly. He was glad to find that a night's rest had also cheered up the others. Barnard could joke happily about the beds, baths, breakfasts, and other comforts. Miss Brinklow admitted that even her most thorough search of her room had failed to find any of the problems she'd been ready for. Even Mallinson had developed a sort of half-sulky acceptance. "I suppose we won't get away today after all," he muttered, "unless somebody moves very quickly about it. These people are typically Oriental—you can't get them to do anything quickly and efficiently."

Conway accepted the comment. Mallinson had been out of England just under a year—long enough, no doubt, to make sweeping statements that he'd probably still be making after twenty years. And it was true, to some extent. Yet to Conway it didn't seem that Eastern people were unusually slow, but rather that Englishmen and Americans rushed around the world in a constant and rather ridiculous state of fever. It was a view he hardly expected any other Westerner to share, but he believed it more strongly as he grew older and more experienced. Then again, it was true that Chang was clever at avoiding direct answers and that Mallinson had good reason to be impatient. Conway wished slightly that he could feel impatient too; it would have been easier for the young man.

He said: "I think we'd better wait and see what today brings. It was probably too optimistic to expect them to do anything last night."

Mallinson looked up sharply. "I suppose you think I made a fool of myself, being so pushy? I couldn't help it—I thought that Chinese fellow was extremely suspicious, and I still do. Did you manage to get any straight answers from him after I went to bed?"

"We didn't talk long. He was vague and indirect about most things."

"We'll have to keep him on track today."

"No doubt," agreed Conway, without much enthusiasm for the idea. "Meanwhile this is an excellent breakfast." It consisted of grapefruit, tea, and flatbread, perfectly prepared and served. Near the end of the meal Chang entered and with a slight bow began exchanging polite greetings which, in English, sounded a bit formal and stiff. Conway would have preferred to talk in Chinese, but so far he hadn't revealed that he spoke any Eastern languages; he felt it might be useful to keep that secret. He listened seriously to Chang's courtesies and assured him he had slept well and felt much better. Chang expressed his pleasure at that and added: "Truly, as your national poet says, sleep knits up the raveled sleeve of care."

This show of learning wasn't well received. Mallinson answered with the scorn any healthy-minded young Englishman must feel at the mention of poetry. "I assume you mean Shakespeare, though I don't know that quote. But I know another one that says 'Stand not upon the order of your going, but go at once.' Without being rude, that's rather what we'd all like to do. And I want to look for those porters right away—this morning, if you don't mind."

The Chinese took this ultimatum calmly, eventually answering: "I am sorry to tell you that it would not be useful. I'm afraid we have no men available who would be willing to travel so far from their homes."

"But good God, man, you don't think we're going to accept that as an answer, do you?"

"I am sincerely sorry, but I can suggest no other."

"You seem to have figured it all out since last night," Barnard put in. "You weren't nearly so certain about things then."

"I didn't want to disappoint you when you were so tired from your journey. Now, after a refreshing night's sleep, I hope you will see things more reasonably."

And so they found themselves no closer to leaving than before, caught between Chang's polite evasiveness and the growing realization that Shangri-La might not be so easy to leave as they had imagined.

CHAPTER 5

They spent the rest of the morning talking about their situation. It was pretty shocking to think that instead of being back in their comfortable lives in Peshawur, they were facing two whole months stuck in a Tibetan monastery. But after everything they'd been through—the hijacking, the crazy flight over the mountains, the pilot's death—they were almost too exhausted to be angry or surprised anymore. Even Mallinson, after his first outburst, settled into a kind of stunned acceptance.

"I'm done arguing about it, Conway," he said, nervously fiddling with a cigarette. "You know how I feel. I've said all along that something's really weird about this whole thing. It's sketchy. I wish I could get out of here right now."

"I don't blame you for feeling that way," Conway replied. "Unfortunately, it's not about what any of us want—it's about what we have to deal with. If these people say they can't or won't give us the porters we need to leave, we're stuck here until help comes. I hate to admit we're this helpless, but that's the truth."

"So you're saying we have to stay here for two months?"

"I don't see what else we can do."

Mallinson flicked his cigarette ash with forced casualness. "Fine then. Two months it is. Now let's all cheer about it."

Conway continued: "I don't see why it should be much worse than being stuck anywhere else in the world. People in our jobs get sent to weird places all the time—that's true for all of us. Of course it's rough for those of us with family and friends back home. Personally, I'm lucky that way—I can't think of anyone who'll be super worried about me, and whatever work I was supposed to do can easily be handled by someone else."

He looked at the others, inviting them to share their own situations. Mallinson didn't say anything, but Conway knew roughly how things stood with him. He had parents and a girlfriend in England; this was going to be really hard on him.

Barnard, on the other hand, seemed to take it all in stride, with what Conway had come to see as his usual good humor. "Well, I guess I'm pretty lucky too—two months in jail won't kill me. As for folks back home, they won't lose any sleep over it—I've always been terrible at keeping in touch anyway."

"You're forgetting that our names will be in the news," Conway reminded him. "We'll be listed as missing, and people will assume the worst."

Barnard looked startled for a moment, then replied with a slight grin: "Oh yeah, that's true, but it doesn't affect me, trust me."

Conway was glad it didn't, though something about that seemed odd. He turned to Miss Brinklow, who had been surprisingly quiet; she hadn't offered any opinion during their talk with Chang. He figured she probably had fewer personal worries too. She said brightly: "Like Mr. Barnard says, two months here is nothing to make a fuss about. It's all the same, wherever you are, when you're doing the Lord's work. Providence has brought me here. I see it as a calling."

Conway thought that was a pretty convenient way to look at it. "I'm sure," he said encouragingly, "your mission society will be impressed when you finally return. You'll have lots of useful information to share. We'll all have had quite an experience, actually. That's one small bright side."

They all started talking more generally then. Conway was kind of surprised at how easily Barnard and Miss Brinklow had accepted their situation. He was relieved, though; it meant he only had one unhappy person to deal with. Even Mallinson, after all the arguing, was starting to calm down. He was still upset, but trying harder to see the positive side. "Who knows what we'll do with ourselves," he said, and just the fact that he was thinking about that showed he was trying to accept things.

"The first rule has to be not getting on each other's nerves," Conway replied. "Luckily, this place seems huge, and there aren't many people around. Except for the servants, we've only seen one person who actually lives here."

Barnard found another reason to be optimistic. "Well, at least we won't starve, judging by the meals we've had so far. You know, Conway, this place isn't run on pocket change. Those baths, for instance—they cost serious money. And I can't see how anyone here earns anything, unless those people in the valley have jobs, and even then, they couldn't produce enough to export. I wonder if they have some kind of mining operation."

"This whole place is just weird," Mallinson responded. "They probably have tons of money hidden away somewhere, like the Jesuits. As for the baths, some rich supporter probably donated them. Anyway, I won't care once I get out of here. Though I have to admit, the view is pretty amazing. It'd make an awesome winter sports center if it was somewhere else. I wonder if you could ski on some of those slopes up there?"

Conway gave him an amused but searching look. "Yesterday, when I found some edelweiss, you reminded me this isn't the Alps. Now it's my turn to say the same thing. I wouldn't try any of your fancy ski moves in this part of the world."

"I bet nobody here has ever even seen a ski jump."

"Or even an ice hockey match," Conway teased back. "Maybe you could start some teams. How about 'Monks versus Visitors'?"

"It would certainly teach them good sportsmanship," Miss Brinklow added with complete seriousness.

That might have been awkward to respond to, but luckily lunch was about to be served. The food was so good and arrived so promptly that everyone felt a bit better. Afterward, when Chang came in, no one wanted to continue arguing. Very tactfully, Chang acted like everything was fine between them all, and they let him think that. In fact, when he offered to show them more of the monastery buildings and act as their guide, they quickly agreed. "Sure thing," said Barnard. "Might as well check the place out while we're here. I doubt any of us will ever visit again."

Miss Brinklow struck a more thoughtful note. "When we left Baskul in that airplane, I never dreamed we'd end up in a place like this," she said as they all followed Chang.

"And we still don't know why we're here," Mallinson added, not quite ready to let it go.

Conway didn't have any prejudices about race or culture, though sometimes he pretended to care about such things when he was around certain people back in India—it was just easier that way. But in China, where he'd had many Chinese friends, he'd never thought of treating them as anything less than equals. So when he talked with Chang, he saw him simply as a well-mannered older gentleman who was very intelligent, even if he might not be completely trustworthy.

Mallinson, however, acted like Chang was some kind of zoo exhibit; Miss Brinklow spoke to him like she was a teacher talking to someone who needed to be educated; and Barnard treated him like a butler. Meanwhile, Chang led them on what turned out to be quite an amazing tour of Shangri-La.

It wasn't the first monastery Conway had ever visited, but it was definitely the biggest and most impressive. Just walking through all the rooms and courtyards was like an afternoon workout, and Conway could tell that Chang wasn't even showing them everything—there were whole buildings they didn't go into. Still, they saw enough for everyone to form their own opinions. Barnard became even more convinced that the monks were rich; Miss Brinklow found plenty of evidence that they were immoral (though she didn't explain why she thought this). Mallinson, after getting over his initial amazement, found himself as tired as he usually got on sightseeing trips at lower altitudes. He decided he probably wasn't going to like the monks very much.

Conway, though, found himself completely enchanted. It wasn't any one thing that attracted him—it was the way everything came together so perfectly, with such amazing taste and harmony. The whole place had this incredible feeling of peace. He had to make himself stop just enjoying it like an artist and start looking at things like someone who knows about art. When he did, he realized they had treasures that museums would fight over—beautiful blue pottery from the Sung dynasty, thousand-year-old paintings done with colored inks, and incredibly detailed lacquer work that looked like it came from a fairy tale.

It was like finding a whole world of perfect, delicate things that had somehow survived through time, stirring up feelings before dissolving into pure thought. There was nothing showy about it, no attempt to impress visitors or make a big deal about how special everything was. These beautiful things seemed to have appeared as naturally as flower petals falling from a flower. Any collector would have gone crazy seeing all this, but Conway didn't collect things—he didn't have the money or the desire to own stuff. He just appreciated Chinese art with his mind; in a world that kept getting noisier and bigger, he liked quiet, precise, small things. As he walked through room after room, he felt a bit sad thinking about how this peaceful place existed right next to the massive, threatening mountain of Karakal.

But the monastery had more surprises in store. One of them was an amazing library—tall and spacious, with so many books tucked away in little alcoves that it felt more like a place of wisdom than just learning, more about good manners than serious study. Conway, taking a quick look at some of the shelves, found lots of things that amazed him. They had the world's best literature, plus tons of rare and interesting books he'd never seen before. There were books in English, French, German, Russian, Chinese, and other Asian languages. He was especially interested in their collection about Tibet—he noticed several super rare books, including some really old ones from the 1600s and 1700s.

He was looking at one of these when he noticed Chang watching him curiously. "Are you a scholar?" Chang asked.

Conway found this hard to answer. His time teaching at Oxford gave him some right to say yes, but he knew that while being called a scholar was a huge compliment from a Chinese person, it sounded kind of stuck-up to English ears. Mostly to avoid embarrassing his companions, he downplayed it. "I enjoy reading, of course," he said, "but my work in recent years hasn't given me much chance for serious study."

"But you wish you had more time for it?"

"Oh, I wouldn't say that exactly, but I definitely see the appeal."

Mallinson, who had picked up a book, interrupted: "Here's something for your studying, Conway. It's a map of this region."

"We have hundreds of maps," said Chang. "They're all available for you to look at, but I should probably tell you one thing right away: you won't find Shangri-La marked on any of them."

"That's strange," Conway commented. "I wonder why?"

"There's a very good reason, but I'm afraid that's all I can say."

Conway smiled, but Mallinson looked annoyed again. "Still keeping up the mystery," he said. "So far we haven't seen much that anyone would need to keep secret."

Suddenly Miss Brinklow spoke up, sounding like a tourist guide who wasn't going to be ignored: "Aren't you going to show us the monks at work?"

One could tell she probably had vague ideas about native crafts —maybe prayer mat weaving or something "picturesque" she could talk about when she got home. She had this amazing ability to never seem very surprised by anything, while always managing to seem slightly disapproving. Chang's response didn't change either of these attitudes: "I'm sorry to say that's impossible. The lamas are never—or perhaps I should say only very rarely—seen by outsiders."

"Well, that's too bad," agreed Barnard. "But it's a real shame. I would've loved to shake hands with your boss."

Chang acknowledged this with serious politeness. Miss Brinklow, however, wasn't done with her questions. "What do the lamas do?" she continued.

"They devote themselves, madam, to contemplation and the pursuit of wisdom."

"But that isn't doing anything."

"Then, madam, they do nothing."

"I thought as much." She found a way to sum it all up. "Well, Mr. Chang, it's very nice being shown all these things, but you won't convince me that a place like this does any real good. I prefer something more practical."

"Perhaps you would like some tea?"

At first Conway thought Chang might be being sarcastic, but it turned out he wasn't; the afternoon had flown by, and Chang, though he didn't eat much, loved drinking tea at regular times like most Chinese people. Miss Brinklow admitted that visiting art galleries and museums always gave her a headache anyway. So everyone agreed to the suggestion, and followed Chang through several courtyards until they came upon something that took their breath away.

From a columned walkway, steps led down to a garden where something magical had been created: a pool full of lotus flowers, their leaves packed so tightly together they looked like a floor of wet green tiles. Around the pool stood bronze statues of lions, dragons, and unicorns—each one looking fierce in a way that somehow made the peaceful garden seem even more peaceful. The whole scene was so perfectly arranged that you could look at it forever without getting tired; nothing seemed to be competing for attention. Even the peak of Karakal, rising above the blue-tiled roofs, seemed to have found its place in this perfect picture.

"Nice little spot," commented Barnard. Chang led them into an open pavilion which, to Conway's increasing amazement, contained both an old-fashioned harpsichord and a modern grand piano. Conway found this perhaps the most surprising thing yet. Chang answered all his questions honestly up to a point; the lamas, he explained, really appreciated Western music, especially Mozart. They had recordings of all the great European compositions, and some of them were skilled musicians themselves.

Barnard was most impressed by how they'd managed to transport everything here. "Are you telling me this piano came up that same path we used yesterday?"

"There is no other way."

"Well, that beats everything! Why, with a radio and a record player, you'd have the complete setup! Though maybe you're not familiar with modern music yet?"

"Oh yes, we've heard about it, but we've been advised that the mountains would make radio reception impossible. As for a record player, the suggestion has already been discussed by the authorities, but they haven't felt any need to rush into getting one."

"I'd believe that even if you hadn't told me," Barnard shot back. "I guess that must be your motto here—'No hurry.'" He laughed loudly and continued: "Well, getting down to details, suppose someday your bosses decide they do want a record player—what happens then? The manufacturers won't deliver here, that's for sure. I bet you have an agent in Peking or Shanghai or somewhere, and I bet everything costs a fortune by the time it gets here."

But Chang was as mysterious about this as he'd been about other things. "Your guesses are clever, Mr. Barnard, but I'm afraid I can't discuss them."

So there they were again, Conway thought, dancing around the edge of what could and couldn't be revealed. But before he could think about it too much, something new caught his attention. While servants were bringing in small bowls of fragrant tea, a girl in Chinese dress had quietly entered. She went straight to the harpsichord and began playing a gavotte by Rameau. The first magical notes stirred something deep in Conway; those delicate French tunes from the eighteenth century seemed to match perfectly with the ancient vases and beautiful lacquerwork and the lotus pool outside. They shared the same timeless beauty, surviving through ages that should have destroyed them. Then he noticed the player herself. She had the long, narrow nose, high cheekbones, and pale complexion of someone from Manchuria; her black hair was pulled back tightly and braided; she looked as delicate and perfect as a miniature painting. Her mouth was like a tiny pink flower, and she sat completely still except for her long, graceful fingers. As soon as the gavotte ended, she bowed slightly and left.

Chang smiled after her and then, with a hint of personal pride, at Conway. "Did you enjoy that?" he asked.

"Who is she?" Mallinson asked before Conway could reply.

"Her name is Lo-Tsen. She is very skilled with Western keyboard music. Like myself, she has not yet reached full initiation."

"I should think not!" exclaimed Miss Brinklow. "She looks hardly more than a child. So you have women lamas too, then?"

"We make no distinctions between men and women here."

"Strange business, this lamahood of yours," Mallinson commented loftily after a pause. The rest of the tea-drinking went on without conversation; echoes of the harpsichord seemed to linger in the air, creating an odd spell. Finally, as they were getting ready to leave the pavilion, Chang said he hoped they had enjoyed the tour. Conway, answering for everyone, balanced politeness with honesty. Chang then assured them they had given him equal pleasure, and hoped they would feel free to use the music room and library throughout their stay. Conway thanked him again, this time more sincerely. "But what about the lamas?" he added. "Don't they ever want to use them?"

"They are happy to give way to their honored guests."

"Well, that's what I call real generous," said Barnard. "And what's more, it shows that the lamas do know we exist. That's progress, anyway—makes me feel more at home. You've certainly got a nice setup here, Chang, and that little girl of yours plays the piano very nicely. How old would she be, I wonder?"

"I'm afraid I cannot tell you."

Barnard laughed. "You don't give away secrets about a lady's age, is that it?"

That evening, after dinner, Conway left the others and went for a walk in the moonlit courtyards. Shangri-La was beautiful at night, touched with a special kind of mystery that lives at the heart of all beautiful things. The air was cold and still; the huge peak of Karakal looked closer than it did during the day. Conway felt physically happy, emotionally content, and mentally at peace—but in his logical mind, which wasn't quite the same thing, something was bothering him. He was puzzled. The line between what the monks would and wouldn't tell them was becoming clearer, but it only revealed more mysteries behind it. The whole amazing series of events that had happened to him and his three random companions was starting to come into focus; he couldn't understand it yet, but he believed it could be understood.

Walking along a covered walkway, he came to a terrace that looked out over the valley. The scent of tuberose flowers filled the air—in China, they called it 'the smell of moonlight.' Conway thought with amusement that if moonlight had a sound, it might be that Rameau gavotte he'd heard earlier. That made him think of the young Manchu girl. He hadn't expected to find women at Shangri-La; you didn't usually associate them with monasteries. Still, he thought, it might not be a bad change to tradition; after all, a female harpsichord player could be a nice addition to any community that was willing to be (in Chang's words) 'moderately unorthodox.'

He looked over the edge into the blue-black emptiness. The drop was unreal—maybe as much as a mile. He wondered if they would let him climb down it and explore the valley civilization they'd mentioned. The idea of this strange pocket of culture, hidden among unknown mountain ranges and ruled by some mysterious group of lamas, interested him as someone who studied history, apart from all the other secrets of the monastery.

Suddenly, carried on a gust of wind, came sounds from far below. Listening carefully, he could hear gongs and trumpets and also (though maybe he was imagining it) the mass of voices chanting. The sounds faded when the wind changed, then came back again. But these hints of life and activity in those hidden depths only made Shangri-La itself feel more peaceful. Its empty courtyards and pale pavilions seemed to float in a calm from which all life's worries had drained away, leaving a silence where moments barely dared to pass. Then, from a window high above the terrace, he caught the rose-gold glow of lantern light; was it there that the lamas devoted themselves to thinking and searching for wisdom? Were they doing that right now? It seemed like he could solve these mysteries just by walking through the nearest door and exploring until he found the truth—but he knew that freedom was an illusion, and that his movements were being watched. Two Tibetans had quietly crossed the terrace and were standing casually near the wall. They looked like friendly guys, adjusting their colored cloaks carelessly over one shoulder.

The whisper of gongs and trumpets rose again, and Conway heard one of the men ask his companion a question. The answer came: "They have buried Talu." Conway, who knew just a little Tibetan, hoped they would keep talking; he couldn't understand much from just one comment. After a pause, the questioner, who Conway couldn't hear clearly, continued the conversation and got answers that Conway loosely understood as:

"He died outside."

"He obeyed the high ones of Shangri-La."

"He came through the air over the great mountains with a bird to hold him."

"Strangers he brought also."

"Talu was not afraid of the outside wind, nor of the outside cold."

"Though he went outside long ago, the valley of Blue Moon remembers him still."

They said nothing else that Conway could understand, and after waiting a while, he went back to his room. He had heard enough to unlock another part of the mystery, and it fit so well that he wondered why he hadn't figured it out himself. The thought had crossed his mind, but it had seemed too fantastic to believe. Now he realized that the fantastic explanation had to be accepted. That flight from Baskul hadn't been the meaningless act of a madman. It had been something planned and carried out under orders from Shangri-La. The dead pilot was known by name to those who lived here; he had been one of them, in some way; they were mourning his death. Everything pointed to some high intelligence directing events for its own purposes; there had been, as it were, a single arch of intention spanning those unexplainable hours and miles. But what was that intention? For what possible reason would four random passengers in a British Government airplane be brought to these remote

JAMES HILTON

Himalayan heights?

Conway was somewhat shocked by the problem, but not entirely unhappy with it. It challenged him in the only way he was really open to being challenged—by touching a certain clarity of mind that only needed a big enough puzzle to solve. He decided one thing right away: the cold thrill of discovery shouldn't be shared yet—not with his companions, who couldn't help him, nor with their hosts, who obviously wouldn't.

CHAPTER 6

"I guess some people have to get used to worse places," Barnard said after their first week at Shangri-La. And he was probably right.

By then, they had settled into a daily routine, and with Chang's help, they weren't as bored as they might have been. They'd gotten used to the thin air and found it actually made them feel pretty good as long as they didn't try anything too strenuous. They learned that the days were warm and the nights cold, that the monastery was protected from winds, that avalanches on Karakal happened most often around noon, that the valley grew good tobacco, and that some of the local food and drinks were better than others. They also learned a lot about each other, like four new students at a school where everyone else was mysteriously absent.

Chang worked hard to make everything comfortable for them. He took them on trips, suggested things to do, recommended books, and kept conversations going at meals whenever things got awkward. He was always kind, polite, and resourceful. It became very clear which questions he would answer and which he wouldn't, and everyone except Mallinson had stopped getting annoyed about the stuff he wouldn't discuss.

Conway just made note of these things, adding them to all

the other clues he was collecting. Barnard even joked with Chang like they were at some American business convention. "You know, Chang, this is a pretty bad hotel. Don't you ever get newspapers here? I'd trade all the books in your library for today's Herald-Tribune."

Chang always answered seriously, though you couldn't always tell if he took every question seriously. "We have complete collections of The Times up until a few years ago," he replied. "But only, I'm sorry to say, the London Times."

Conway was glad to find out they were allowed to visit the valley, though it was too difficult to go down there without guides. With Chang, they spent a whole day exploring the green valley floor that looked so beautiful from the cliff edge. Conway found it fascinating. They traveled in bamboo chairs carried by porters, swinging over scary drops while the carriers picked their way carefully down the steep path. It wasn't a route for anyone afraid of heights, but when they finally reached the lower levels of forest and hills, they could see why the monastery's location was so perfect.

The valley was like an enclosed paradise, incredibly fertile, where just a few thousand feet of elevation difference created a whole range of climates from temperate to tropical. All kinds of different crops grew close together, with every inch of ground carefully tended. The whole cultivated area stretched for maybe twelve miles, between one and five miles wide, and though it was narrow, it caught the sun at the hottest part of the day. The air was pleasantly warm even in the shade, though the little streams that watered the soil were ice-cold from the mountain snow. Looking up at the massive mountain wall, Conway felt again that there was something both beautiful and dangerous about the scene; if it weren't for some chance-placed barrier, the whole valley would clearly have been a lake, constantly filled by the glaciers around it. Instead, a few streams trickled through to fill reservoirs and water fields and plantations as carefully as if planned by an expert engineer. The whole setup was almost unbelievably perfect, as long as no earthquake or landslide disturbed it.

But even these vague future worries only made the present more beautiful. Once again Conway found himself captivated, just as he had during his happiest years in China. The huge mountains made a perfect contrast with the tiny lawns and perfectly kept gardens, the painted tea houses by the streams, and the delicate-looking houses. The people seemed to him a very successful mix of Chinese and Tibetan; they were cleaner and better-looking than the average of either group, and showed no signs of problems from the inevitable inbreeding in such a small community. They smiled and laughed as they passed the visitors in their chairs, and had friendly words for Chang. They were good-humored and mildly curious, polite and carefree, busy with many jobs but never seeming to rush.

Conway thought they were one of the nicest communities he'd ever seen. Even Miss Brinklow, who had been watching for signs of "pagan degradation," had to admit that everything looked very good "on the surface." She was relieved to find the natives "completely" dressed, even though the women wore Chinese-style trousers, and her most imaginative inspection of a Buddhist temple only revealed a few items she found questionable. Chang explained that the temple had its own lamas, who were loosely supervised by Shangri-La but weren't part of the same order. There were also Taoist and Confucian temples further along the valley. "The jewel has many faces," said Chang, "and it's possible that many religions are moderately true."

"I agree with that," said Barnard enthusiastically. "I never believed in religious jealousy. Chang, you're a philosopher—I'll have to remember what you said. 'Many religions are moderately true'—I figure you guys up on the mountain are pretty smart to have figured that out. You're right too—I'm sure of it."

"But we," responded Chang dreamily, "are only moderately sure."

Miss Brinklow couldn't be bothered with all that, which seemed to her just laziness. She had her own idea anyway. "When I get back," she said firmly, "I'm going to ask my mission society to send a missionary here. And if they complain about the cost, I'll just keep pushing until they agree."

That was clearly a much healthier attitude, and even Mallinson, who didn't care much for foreign missions, had to admire her determination. "They should send you," he said. "That is, of course, if you'd like a place like this."

"It's hardly about liking it," Miss Brinklow shot back. "One wouldn't like it, naturally—how could one? It's about what one feels one ought to do."

"I think," said Conway, "if I were a missionary, I'd choose this over quite a lot of other places."

"In that case," snapped Miss Brinklow, "there would be no virtue in it, obviously."

"But I wasn't thinking about virtue."

"More's the pity, then. There's no good in doing something just because you like doing it. Look at these people here!"

"They all seem very happy."

"Exactly," she answered fiercely. She added: "Anyway, I don't see why I shouldn't make a start by learning the language. Can you lend me a book about it, Mr. Chang?"

Chang was at his most polite. "Most certainly, madam—with the greatest pleasure. And, if I may say so, I think the idea is excellent."

When they went back up to Shangri-La that evening, he treated it as something really important. Miss Brinklow was a bit intimidated at first by the huge book he gave her (written by a German scholar in the 1800s—she'd probably expected something more like "Quick and Easy Tibetan"). But with help from Chang and encouragement from Conway, she made a good start and soon seemed to be getting real satisfaction from the challenge.

Conway found plenty to interest him too, apart from the mystery he was trying to solve. During the warm, sunny days, he spent a lot of time in the library and music room, and became more and more impressed by how cultured the lamas were. They had incredibly varied taste in books—you could find Plato next to Omar Khayyam, Nietzsche beside Newton. Conway estimated there were between twenty and thirty thousand books, and he wondered how they chose which ones to get and how they got them here. He also tried to figure out how recently they'd gotten new books, but the newest one he could find was a cheap copy of "All Quiet on the Western Front." Later, though, Chang told him they had other books published up until about the middle of 1930 that would eventually be added to the shelves—they'd already arrived at the monastery. "We keep fairly up-to-date, you see," he commented.

"Some people might disagree with you," Conway replied with a smile. "Quite a lot has happened in the world since last year, you know."

"Nothing important that couldn't have been predicted in 1920, or that won't be better understood in 1940."

"So you're not interested in the latest developments of the world crisis?"

"I'll be very interested—in due time."

"You know, Chang, I think I'm starting to understand you. You're on a different schedule—time means less to you than it does to most people. If I were in London, I wouldn't always be desperate to see the newest newspaper, and here at Shangri-La, you're not desperate to see one from a year ago. Both attitudes make sense to me."

Conway enjoyed these conversations with Chang, even though he still found it strange that he met so few other people from the monastery. Apart from the lamas themselves, who seemed to be off-limits, weren't there other students besides Chang?

Well, there was the young Manchu girl. He sometimes saw her when he visited the music room, but she didn't speak English, and he still didn't want to reveal that he knew Chinese. He couldn't tell if she played music just for fun or if she was studying. She was very formal in everything she did, and she always chose very structured music—Bach, Corelli, Scarlatti, and sometimes Mozart. She preferred the harpsichord to the piano, but when Conway played the piano, she would listen with serious, almost dutiful appreciation. It was impossible to know what she was thinking, and even hard to guess her age. He thought she could be anywhere from thirteen to thirty, and somehow neither seemed completely impossible.

Mallinson, who sometimes came to listen to the music because there wasn't much else to do, found her puzzling. "I can't figure out what she's doing here," he said to Conway more than once. "This lama business might make sense for an old guy like Chang, but what's the appeal for a girl? How long has she been here, I wonder?"

"I wonder too, but that's one of those things they probably won't tell us."

"Do you think she likes being here?"

"Well, she doesn't seem to dislike it."

"She doesn't seem to have any feelings at all. She's more like a little ivory doll than a real person."

"That's not such a bad thing to be like."

"As far as it goes."

Conway smiled. "And it goes pretty far, Mallinson, when you think about it. After all, she has good manners, good taste in clothes, looks nice, plays the harpsichord beautifully, and moves gracefully around a room. From what I remember of Western Europe, quite a lot of girls there don't have any of those qualities."

"You're really cynical about women, Conway."

Conway was used to being called cynical. He hadn't actually had much to do with women, and during his leaves in Indian hill stations, it had been easy to get a reputation as a cynic. The truth was, he'd had several wonderful friendships with women who would have been happy to marry him if he'd asked—but he hadn't asked. He'd once almost gotten as far as announcing his engagement in the Morning Post, but the girl didn't want to live in Peking and he didn't want to live in Tunbridge Wells, and neither would change their mind. His experience with women had been tentative, occasional, and somewhat inconclusive. But he wasn't really cynical about them.

He laughed. "I'm thirty-seven—you're twenty-four. That's all it comes down to."

After a pause, Mallinson suddenly asked: "By the way, how old would you say Chang is?"

"Anything," Conway replied lightly, "between forty-nine and a hundred and forty-nine."

Even though Chang wouldn't answer all their questions, he was happy to share lots of other information. He was particularly open about how the valley people lived, and Conway, who was interested in how different societies worked, had long talks with him that could have filled a college paper. He was especially curious about how the valley was governed; it turned out to be a pretty relaxed system run from the monastery with a light touch that somehow worked perfectly. The valley was clearly successful—you could see that every time you went down there.

Conway was puzzled about how they kept law and order; there didn't seem to be any soldiers or police, but surely they must have some way of dealing with troublemakers? Chang explained that crime was very rare, partly because they only considered really serious things crimes, and partly because everyone had enough of everything they could reasonably want. In the worst cases, the monastery's servants had the power to kick someone out of the valley—though this punishment, which everyone considered terrible, had only been used a few times.

But the main way they governed Blue Moon Valley, Chang explained, was by teaching good manners, which made people feel certain things just weren't done, and that they'd lose respect by doing them. "You English do the same thing in your private schools," said Chang, "but not for the same things. Our valley people, for instance, feel it's 'not done' to be unfriendly to strangers, to argue angrily, or to try to get ahead of each other. The idea of enjoying what your English headmasters call the pretend warfare of sports would seem completely barbaric to them—just pointlessly stirring up all the worst instincts."

Conway asked if they ever had fights over women.

"Very rarely, because it wouldn't be considered good manners to take a woman another man wanted."

"What if someone wanted her so badly they didn't care about good manners?"

"Then, my dear sir, it would be good manners for the other man to let him have her, and for the woman to agree too. You'd be surprised how applying a little courtesy all around helps solve these problems."

During his visits to the valley, Conway found a spirit of goodwill and contentment that impressed him all the more because he knew that of all human skills, governing well was the hardest to perfect. When he complimented Chang about this, he responded: "Ah, but you see, we believe that to govern perfectly it's necessary to avoid governing too much."

"But you don't have any democratic system—voting, and so on?"

"Oh no. Our people would be quite shocked by having to declare that one policy was completely right and another completely wrong."

Conway smiled. He found that attitude pretty appealing.

Meanwhile, Miss Brinklow found her own satisfaction in studying Tibetan; meanwhile Mallinson kept complaining and worrying; and meanwhile Barnard maintained a cheerfulness that seemed almost as strange as everything else about their situation.

"To tell you the truth," said Mallinson, "the guy's cheerfulness is really getting on my nerves. I understand trying to keep a stiff upper lip, but his constant joking around is starting to upset me. He'll be the life of the party if we don't watch out."

Conway had wondered himself about how easily the American had settled in. He replied: "Isn't it lucky for us that he takes things so well?"

"I think it's weird. What do you know about him, Conway? I mean who he is, and all that?"

"Not much more than you do. I knew he came from Persia and was supposed to be looking for oil. It's his way to take things easily—when we arranged the air evacuation, I had to work hard to convince him to join us. He only agreed when I told him an American passport wouldn't stop a bullet."

"By the way, did you ever see his passport?"

"Probably, but I don't remember. Why?"

Mallinson laughed. "I'm afraid you'll think I've been nosy. But why shouldn't I be? Two months in this place should reveal all our secrets, if we have any. Actually, it was a complete accident how I found out, and I haven't told anyone else, of course. I wasn't even going to tell you, but since we're talking about it..."

"Yes, of course, but I wish you'd tell me what you're talking about."

"Just this. Barnard was traveling on a fake passport, and he isn't Barnard at all."

Conway raised his eyebrows with interest, though not really concern. He liked Barnard, as much as he felt strongly about anyone, but it was impossible for him to care intensely about who the man really was or wasn't. He asked: "Well, who do you think he is, then?"

"He's Chalmers Bryant."

"Really! What makes you think so?"

"He dropped a wallet this morning and Chang picked it up and gave it to me, thinking it was mine. I couldn't help seeing it was full of newspaper clippings—some fell out while I was handling it, and I'll admit I looked at them. After all, newspaper clippings aren't private, or shouldn't be. They were all about Bryant and the search for him, and one of them had a photograph that looked exactly like Barnard except for a mustache."

"Did you mention what you found to Barnard himself?"

"No, I just gave him back his wallet without saying anything."

"So this whole thing is based on you recognizing a newspaper photo?"

"Well, so far, yes."

"I wouldn't want to convict anyone based just on that. Of course you might be right—I'm not saying he couldn't be Bryant. If he is, it would explain why he's so happy being here—he could hardly find a better hiding place."

Mallinson seemed disappointed that Conway wasn't more shocked by this news. "Well, what are you going to do about it?" he asked.

Conway thought for a moment and then answered: "I don't have much of an idea. Probably nothing at all. What can we do, anyway?"

"But come on, if he's Bryant—"

"My dear Mallinson, if he were Nero it wouldn't matter to us right now! Saint or crook, we have to make the best of each other's company while we're here, and I don't think we'll help anything by making a big deal about it. If I'd suspected who he was at Baskul, I would have tried to contact Delhi about him—it would have been my duty. But now I think I can say I'm off duty."

"Don't you think that's a pretty lazy way to look at it?"

"I don't care if it's lazy as long as it makes sense."

"I suppose that means you want me to forget what I found out?"

"You probably can't do that, but I definitely think we should both keep it to ourselves. Not to protect Barnard or Bryant or whoever he is, but to avoid making things really awkward until we leave."

"You mean we should just let him go?"

"Well, I'll put it differently and say we should let someone else have the pleasure of catching him. When you've lived quite normally with someone for a few months, it seems a bit out of place to suddenly call for handcuffs."

"I don't agree. The man's nothing but a huge thief—I know lots of people who lost their money because of him."

Conway shrugged. He admired how clear-cut Mallinson's values were; the private-school ethics might be simple, but at least they were straightforward. If someone broke the law, it was everyone's duty to turn them in—as long as it was the kind of law you weren't allowed to break. And the law about checks and stocks and balance sheets was definitely that kind. Bryant had broken it, and though Conway hadn't paid much attention to the case, he had a feeling it was one of the worst of its kind. All he knew was that when Bryant's huge company in New York failed, people lost about a hundred million dollars—a record-breaking crash, even in a world full of records. Somehow (Conway wasn't a financial expert) Bryant had been manipulating things on Wall Street, and the result had been an arrest warrant, his escape to Europe, and orders to arrest him in half a dozen countries.

Conway said finally: "Well, if you take my advice, you'll keep quiet about it—not for his sake but for ours. Do what you want, but don't forget he might not even be the right person."

But he was, and they found out that evening after dinner. Chang had left them; Miss Brinklow was studying her Tibetan grammar; the three men faced each other over coffee and cigars. The conversation during dinner would have died several times if not for Chang's tact and friendliness; now, without him, there was an uncomfortable silence. Barnard wasn't making his usual jokes. Conway could tell that Mallinson couldn't treat the American as if nothing had happened, and he could also tell that Barnard knew something was up.

Suddenly the American threw away his cigar. "I guess you all know who I am," he said.

Mallinson blushed, but Conway replied calmly: "Yes, Mallinson and I think we do."

"Pretty careless of me to leave those clippings lying around."

"We're all careless sometimes."

"Well, you're taking it pretty calmly, that's something."

There was another silence, broken by Miss Brinklow's sharp voice: "I'm sure I don't know who you are, Mr. Barnard, though I must say I guessed all along you were traveling under a false name." They all looked at her curiously and she went on: "I remember when Mr. Conway said we'd all have our names in the papers, you said it didn't affect you. I thought then that Barnard probably wasn't your real name."

The guilty man smiled slowly as he lit another cigar. "Ma'am," he said after a while, "you're not just a good detective, but you've found a really polite way to describe my situation. I'm traveling under a false name. You've said it, and you're absolutely right. As for you boys, I'm not sorry in a way that you've found me out. As long as none of you knew, we could all manage, but considering our situation, it wouldn't be very neighborly to keep pretending now. You folks have been so nice to me that I don't want to cause any trouble. It looks like we're all going to be stuck together for better or worse for a while, and we should help each other as much as we can. As for what happens afterward, I figure we can deal with that when the time comes."

Conway found all this so reasonable that he looked at Barnard with new interest, and even—though it might seem odd at such a moment—a touch of real appreciation. It was strange to think of that heavy, cheerful, rather fatherly-looking man as the world's biggest swindler. He looked more like someone who, with a bit more education, would have made a popular elementary school principal. Behind his good humor you could see signs of recent stress and worry, but that didn't mean the good humor was fake. He was clearly what he seemed—a naturally nice guy who had become a shark only in his professional life.

Conway said: "Yes, that's very much the best thing."

Then Barnard laughed. It was as if he had even deeper reserves of good humor that he could now tap into. "Man, this is weird," he exclaimed, settling back in his chair. "The whole thing, I mean. All across Europe, through Turkey and Persia to that tiny place in the middle of nowhere! Police chasing me the whole time—they nearly caught me in Vienna! Being chased is exciting at first, but it gets on your nerves after a while. I got a good rest at Baskul though—I thought I'd be safe in the middle of a revolution."

"And you were," said Conway with a slight smile, "except from bullets."

"Yeah, and that's what worried me at the end. I can tell you it was a tough choice—whether to stay in Baskul and get shot, or take a ride in your government's plane and find handcuffs waiting at the other end. I wasn't exactly eager to do either."

"I remember you weren't."

Barnard laughed again. "Well, that's how it was, and you can probably figure out that this change of plans doesn't bother me too much. It's a first-class mystery, I'll admit, but for me, personally, there couldn't have been a better one. I don't complain when I'm satisfied."

Conway's smile became more genuine. "A very sensible attitude, though I think you overdid it. We were all starting to wonder how you managed to be so content."

"Well, I was content. This isn't a bad place, once you get used to it. The air's a bit thin at first, but you can't have everything. And it's nice and quiet for a change. Every fall I go to Palm Beach for a rest cure, but they don't really give you one—you're still caught up in all the action. But here I guess I'm getting exactly what the doctor ordered, and it feels great. I'm on a different diet, I can't check the stock market, and my broker can't get me on the phone."

"I bet he wishes he could."

"Sure. There'll be quite a mess to clean up, I don't doubt."

He said this so simply that Conway couldn't help responding: "I'm not much of an expert on what people call high finance."

It was an opening, and the American took it without hesitation. "High finance," he said, "is mostly nonsense."

"That's what I've often thought."

"Look here, Conway, I'll put it like this. A guy does what he's been doing for years, what lots of other guys have been doing, and suddenly the market turns against him. He can't help it, but he keeps his chin up and waits for things to turn around. But somehow they don't turn around like they used to, and after he's lost ten million dollars or so, he reads in some paper that a Swedish professor thinks it's the end of the world. Now I ask you, does that kind of thing help the markets? Of course, it gives him a shock, but he still can't do anything about it. And there he is until the police come—if he waits for them. I didn't."

"You're saying it was all just bad luck, then?"

"Well, I certainly had plenty of that."

"You also had other people's money," Mallinson cut in sharply.

"Yeah, I did. And why? Because they all wanted something for nothing and didn't have the brains to get it themselves."

"I don't agree. It was because they trusted you and thought their money was safe."

"Well, it wasn't safe. It couldn't be. There isn't safety anywhere, and those who thought there was were like people trying to hide under an umbrella in a hurricane."

Conway said peacefully: "Well, we'll all admit you couldn't help the hurricane."

"I couldn't even pretend to help it—any more than you could help what happened after we left Baskul. The same thing struck me when I watched you in the plane staying completely calm while Mallinson here was getting all worked up. You knew you couldn't do anything about it, so you didn't waste energy worrying. Just like I felt when the crash came."

"That's ridiculous!" cried Mallinson. "Anyone can avoid swindling. It's about playing by the rules."

"Which is really hard to do when the whole game is falling apart. Besides, there isn't a person in the world who knows what all the rules are. All the professors at Harvard and Yale couldn't tell you."

Mallinson replied scornfully: "I'm talking about a few simple rules of basic decent behavior."

"Then I reckon your basic decent behavior doesn't include running trust companies."

Conway quickly stepped in. "We'd better not argue. I don't mind the comparison between your situation and mine. No doubt we've all been flying blind lately—both literally and in other ways. But we're here now, that's what matters, and I agree with you that we could be much worse off. You want a rest cure and a hiding place; Miss Brinklow feels called to convert the Tibetans."

"Who's the third person you're counting?" Mallinson interrupted. "Not me, I hope?"

"I was including myself," answered Conway. "And my reason is maybe the simplest of all—I just rather like being here."

Later that evening, when he took his usual solitary walk along the terrace by the lotus pool, Conway felt an extraordinary sense of physical and mental peace. It was absolutely true; he just rather liked being at Shangri-La. Its atmosphere calmed him while its mystery kept his mind interested, and the combination was very pleasant. For several days now he'd been reaching, slowly and carefully, an unusual conclusion about the monastery and its inhabitants; his mind was still working on it, though in a deeper way he felt completely at peace. He was like a mathematician with a complex problem—puzzling over it, but puzzling very calmly and without personal worry.

As for Bryant, whom he decided he'd still think of and call Barnard, the question of his crimes and identity quickly faded into the background, except for one phrase of his—'the whole game is falling apart.' Conway found himself remembering and giving it a wider meaning than the American had probably intended; he felt it applied to Baskul and Delhi and London, to making war and building empires, to consulates and trade agreements and dinner parties at Government House. There was a smell of decay over that whole remembered world, and Barnard's crash had just been more dramatic than his own. The whole game was probably falling apart, but fortunately the players weren't usually put on trial for the pieces they couldn't save. In that way, financiers were unlucky.

But here at Shangri-La, all was deeply calm. The stars filled the moonless sky, and a pale blue light shone on the peak of Karakal. Conway realized then that if by some change of plan the porters from the outside world were to arrive immediately, he wouldn't be completely happy about being rescued so soon. And neither would Barnard, he thought with an inner smile. It was funny, really, and suddenly he knew that he still liked Barnard—otherwise he wouldn't have found it funny. Somehow, stealing a hundred million dollars was almost too big to hold against someone; it would have been easier if he'd just stolen a watch.

Then suddenly, interrupting his thoughts, he became aware of Chang approaching. "Sir," began the Chinese, his slow whisper quickening slightly, "I am proud to be the bearer of important news..."

So the porters had come early, was Conway's first thought; it was strange that he'd just been thinking about that. And he felt the twinge of regret he'd half expected. "Well?" he asked.

Chang was as close to excited as he ever got. "My dear sir, I congratulate you," he continued. "And I'm happy to think I'm partly responsible—it was after my own strong and repeated recommendations that the High Lama made his decision. He wishes to see you immediately."

Conway looked at him quizzically. "You're being less clear than usual, Chang. What's happened?"

"The High Lama has sent for you."

"So I understand. But why all the fuss?"

"Because it's extraordinary and unprecedented—even I who suggested it didn't expect it to happen yet. Two weeks ago you hadn't arrived, and now you're about to be received by him! Never before has it happened so soon!"

"I'm still confused. I understand I'm going to see your High Lama—that's clear enough. But is there something else?"

"Is it not enough?"

Conway laughed. "Absolutely, I assure you—don't think I'm

being rude. Actually, I was thinking of something completely different at first—anyway, never mind about that now. Of course I'll be both honored and delighted to meet him. When is it?"

"Now. I've been sent to bring you to him."

"Isn't it rather late?"

"That doesn't matter. My dear sir, you'll understand many things very soon. And may I add how happy I am personally that this waiting period—which is always awkward—is now over. Believe me, it has been very difficult for me to have to refuse you information so many times—extremely difficult. I'm overjoyed to know that such unpleasantness will never be necessary again."

"You're a strange fellow, Chang," Conway responded. "But let's get going—don't bother explaining any more. I'm perfectly ready and I appreciate your kind words. Lead the way."

CHAPTER 7

Conway stayed calm on the outside, but inside he was buzzing with excitement as he followed Chang across the empty courtyards. If what the Chinese man had said meant anything, Conway was about to find out if his half-formed theory about Shangri-La was as impossible as it seemed.

Apart from that, it would probably be an interesting meeting anyway. He'd met many strange rulers in his time; he found them fascinating and was usually good at figuring them out. He also had a useful talent for saying polite things in languages he barely knew. But this time, he thought, he'd probably do more listening than talking.

He noticed Chang was taking him through rooms he hadn't seen before, all of them dimly lit and beautiful in the lantern light. Then they climbed a spiral staircase to a door where a Tibetan servant was waiting. This part of the monastery, on a higher floor, was as nicely decorated as the rest, but what really struck Conway was how warm and stuffy it was, as if all the windows were sealed tight and some kind of heating system was working overtime. The air got thicker as they went on, until finally Chang stopped at a door that felt like it might lead to a sauna.

"The High Lama," Chang whispered, "will receive you alone." He opened the door for Conway, then closed it behind him so quietly that Conway barely noticed him leave.

Conway stood uncertainly, breathing air that was not only hot but so dark that it took several seconds for his eyes to adjust. Then he slowly made out a dark-curtained room with a low ceiling, simply furnished with a table and chairs. In one of these sat a small, pale, and wrinkled person, sitting so still in the shadows that he looked like an old portrait painting in soft light and dark. There was something about him that seemed both there and not there, with a natural dignity that seemed to come from inside rather than being put on. Conway was fascinated by how strongly he felt all this, and wondered if it was real or just his reaction to the rich, twilight warmth. He felt dizzy under the gaze of those ancient eyes as he took a few steps forward and then stopped.

The person in the chair became clearer now, but hardly more solid-looking. He was a small old man in Chinese clothes that hung loosely on his thin frame. "You are Mr. Conway?" he whispered in perfect English.

The voice was pleasantly calming and touched with a gentle sadness that fell over Conway like a peaceful spell, though again he wondered if the warm air might be partly responsible.

"I am," he answered.

The voice continued: "It is a pleasure to see you, Mr. Conway. I sent for you because I thought we should have a talk. Please sit beside me and don't be afraid. I am an old man and can't harm anyone."

Conway answered: "I feel very honored to be received by you."

"Thank you, my dear Conway—I'll call you that, in your English style. As I said, this is a very pleasant moment for me. My eyesight is poor, but believe me, I can see you in my mind as well as with my eyes. I trust you've been comfortable at Shangri-La since you arrived?"

"Very comfortable."

"I'm glad. Chang has done his best for you, I'm sure. It has been a pleasure for him too. He tells me you've been asking many questions about our community?"

"I am definitely interested in it."

"Then if you can spare some time, I'll be happy to tell you briefly how we were founded."

"I would love nothing more."

"That's what I thought—and hoped... But first, before we begin..."

He made the smallest movement with his hand, and immediately, through some signal Conway couldn't detect, a servant entered to prepare tea. The delicate little cups of almost colorless liquid were placed on a lacquered tray. Conway, who knew the ceremony, took it quite seriously. The voice asked: "Our ways are familiar to you, then?"

Following an impulse he couldn't explain or resist, Conway answered: "I lived in China for several years."

"You didn't tell Chang."

"No."

"Then why do I get this honor?"

Conway was usually good at explaining his own reasons for doing things, but this time he couldn't think of any reason at all. Finally he replied: "To be completely honest, I have no idea, except that I must have wanted to tell you."

"The best of all reasons, I'm sure, between those who are to become friends... Now tell me, isn't this a delicate aroma? China has many fragrant teas, but this one, which is special to our valley, is in my opinion just as good."

Conway lifted his cup and tasted. The flavor was delicate and mysterious, like a ghost of taste that haunted rather than lived on his tongue. He said: "It's wonderful, and completely new to me."

"Yes, like many of our valley's plants, it's both unique and precious. It should be tasted very slowly—not just out of respect and appreciation, but to get the most pleasure from it. This is a famous lesson we can learn from Kou Kai Tchou, who lived about fifteen hundred years ago. He would always wait before eating the sweet center of a piece of sugar cane because, as he explained—'I introduce myself gradually into the region of delights.' Have you studied any of the great Chinese classics?"

Conway replied that he knew a few of them a little. He knew this kind of indirect conversation would continue, according to custom, until they finished their tea. But he didn't mind, even though he was eager to hear about Shangri-La's history. Maybe he had a bit of Kou Kai Tchou's patient appreciation in himself.

Finally, the signal was given mysteriously again, the servant padded in and out, and with no more delay, the High Lama of Shangri-La began:

"You probably know the general outline of Tibetan history, my dear Conway. Chang tells me you've made good use of our library, and I'm sure you've studied the rare but fascinating records of this region. You'll know that Nestorian Christianity spread throughout Asia during the Middle Ages, and its memory lasted long after it disappeared. In the 1600s, Christianity made a comeback through brave Jesuit missionaries whose journeys are much more interesting to read about than St. Paul's. Gradually the Church established itself over a huge area, and it's a remarkable fact, not known by many Europeans today, that for thirty-eight years there was even a Christian mission in Lhasa itself. But it wasn't from Lhasa but from Peking, in 1719, that four Capuchin friars set out looking for any traces of the old Nestorian faith that might still exist in the remote regions.

"They traveled southwest for many months, through Lanchow and the Koko-Nor, facing hardships you can imagine. Three died on the way, and the fourth was close to death when he accidentally stumbled into the rocky pass that's still the only practical way to reach Blue Moon Valley. There, to his joy and surprise, he found friendly and prosperous people who quickly showed what I've always thought of as our oldest tradition—hospitality to strangers. He soon got better and started preaching. The people were Buddhists but willing to listen to him, and he had quite a bit of success. There was an old monastery already here on this mountain shelf, but it was falling apart both physically and spiritually. As the Capuchin gained more followers, he had the idea of building a Christian monastery on this amazing site. Under his supervision, the old buildings were repaired and mostly rebuilt, and he started living here in 1734, when he was fifty-three years old.

"Let me tell you more about this man. His name was Perrault, and he was born in Luxembourg. Before dedicating himself to Far Eastern missions, he had studied at Paris, Bologna, and other universities; he was quite scholarly. We don't have many records of his early life, but it wasn't unusual for someone of his time and profession. He loved music and the arts, was especially good with languages, and before he was sure about becoming a priest, he had experienced all the usual pleasures of the world. The Battle of Malplaquet happened when he was young, and he knew firsthand the horrors of war and invasion. He was physically strong; during his first years here he worked with his hands like anyone else, tending his own garden and learning from the locals while teaching them. He found gold deposits in the valley but wasn't tempted by them; he was more interested in local plants and herbs. He was humble and not rigid in his beliefs. He discouraged having multiple wives, but he saw no reason to ban the popular tangatse berry, which was thought to have medicinal properties but was mainly liked because it had mild narcotic effects. In fact, Perrault became something of a regular user himself; it was his way to accept anything harmless and pleasant from native life, and to give in return the spiritual treasure of the West. He wasn't strict; he enjoyed good things, and was careful to teach his converts cooking as well as religion.

"I want you to picture a rather serious, busy, learned, simple, and enthusiastic person who, along with his priestly duties, wasn't too proud to put on workman's clothes and help build these very rooms. That was, of course, incredibly difficult work, and only his pride and determination could have gotten it done. Pride, I say, because that was definitely a main reason at first—the pride in his own faith that made him decide that if Buddha could inspire people to build a temple on the ledge of Shangri-La, Rome could do just as much.

"But as time passed, it was natural that this motive should gradually give way to calmer ones. Competition is really a young person's spirit, and by the time his monastery was well established, Perrault was already quite old. You should understand that he hadn't, strictly speaking, been following all the rules; though you have to give some leeway to someone whose church superiors were years of travel away rather than just miles. But the valley people and the monks themselves had no doubts; they loved and obeyed him, and as years went by, they came to revere him too. Once in a while he would send reports to the Bishop of Peking, but often they never arrived, and since it was assumed the messengers had died on the dangerous journey, Perrault became more and more unwilling to risk people's lives. After about 1750, he stopped trying. Some of his earlier messages must have gotten through, though, and raised some doubts about what he was doing, because in 1769 a stranger brought a letter that had been written twelve years before, ordering Perrault to come to Rome.

He would have been over seventy if the command had arrived on time; as it was, he was eighty-nine. The long trek over mountains and plateaus was unthinkable; he could never have survived the fierce winds and bitter cold of the wilderness outside. So he sent back a polite reply explaining the situation, but there's no record that his message ever made it past the great mountain ranges.

So Perrault stayed at Shangri-La, not exactly disobeying orders, but because it was physically impossible for him to follow them. Anyway, he was an old man, and death would probably soon solve the problem. By this time, the place he had created had begun to change in subtle ways. This wasn't really surprising; you could hardly expect one man alone to permanently change the habits and traditions of an entire era. He had no Western colleagues to help maintain things when his own influence weakened, and it had probably been a mistake to build on a site that held such different and older memories. It was asking too much; but then again, how could you expect a grey-haired man in his nineties to realize he'd made a mistake? Perrault, at any rate, didn't realize it then. He was far too old and happy. His followers were devoted even when they forgot his teaching, while the valley people loved and respected him so much that he found it easier and easier to forgive them when they went back to their old ways.

He was still active, and his mind had stayed exceptionally sharp. At ninety-eight, he began studying the Buddhist writings that had been left at Shangri-La by its previous occupants, planning to spend the rest of his life writing a book attacking Buddhism from a Christian viewpoint. He actually finished this task (we still have his manuscript), but the attack was very gentle, because by then he had reached a hundred years old—an age when even the strongest disagreements tend to fade.

Meanwhile, as you can imagine, many of his early disciples had died, and since there weren't many new ones, the number of people living under the old Capuchin's rule steadily decreased.

From over eighty at one point, it dropped to twenty, and then to just a dozen, most of them very old themselves. Perrault's life during this time became a very peaceful waiting for the end. He was far too old for illness and unhappiness; only endless sleep could claim him now, and he wasn't afraid. The valley people, out of kindness, provided food and clothing; his library gave him work. He had become rather frail but still had energy for the main ceremonies of his office; the rest of his quiet days he spent with his books, his memories, and the mild pleasures of the narcotic. His mind stayed so incredibly clear that he even started studying certain mystic practices that the Indians call yoga, based on special ways of breathing. For someone his age, this might have seemed dangerous, and it's certainly true that soon afterward, in that memorable year 1789, word spread to the valley that Perrault was finally dying.

"He lay in this very room, my dear Conway, where he could see from the window the white blur that was all his failing eyesight showed him of Karakal; but he could see with his mind too—he could picture the clear, perfect outline that he had first glimpsed half a century before. And all his many experiences came back to him: the years of travel across desert and highland, the huge crowds in Western cities, the noise and glitter of Marlborough's troops. His mind had become as calm as fresh snow; he was ready, willing, and glad to die. He gathered his friends and servants around him and said goodbye to them all; then he asked to be left alone for a while. In this solitude, with his body failing and his mind lifted to a state of joy, he had hoped to give up his soul... but that's not what happened. He lay for many weeks without speaking or moving, and then he began to recover. He was a hundred and eight years old."

The whispering stopped for a moment, and to Conway, moving slightly, it seemed that the High Lama had been translating smoothly from some private dream. Finally, he continued:

"Like others who have waited long at death's door, Perrault had been given a vision to take back with him into the world; and we'll talk more about this vision later. For now, I'll just tell you what he did, which was quite remarkable. Instead of resting quietly as you might expect, he immediately started a strict routine of self-discipline mixed with using the narcotic drug. Taking drugs and doing breathing exercises—it didn't seem like a recipe for cheating death; yet somehow, when the last of the old monks died in 1794, Perrault was still alive.

It might have seemed funny if there had been anyone at Shangri-La with a twisted enough sense of humor. The wrinkled Capuchin, no more frail than he'd been for a dozen years, kept up his secret practice, while to the valley people he became wrapped in mystery—a hermit with strange powers who lived alone on that incredible cliff. But they still felt affection for him, and it became considered good luck to climb to Shangri-La and leave a simple gift or help with some needed task. Perrault blessed all these pilgrims –probably forgetting that they were technically lost sheep from his flock. For 'Te Deum Laudamus' and 'Om Mane Padme Hum' were now heard equally in the valley temples.

As the new century approached, the legend grew into rich and fantastic folklore—people said Perrault had become a god, that he worked miracles, and that on certain nights he flew to the top of Karakal to hold a candle to the sky. There's always a pale glow on the mountain at full moon, but I should tell you that neither Perrault nor any other person has ever climbed up there. I mention this, even though it might seem unnecessary, because there are many unreliable stories about impossible things Perrault supposedly did. People thought, for instance, that he could make himself float in the air, which many

Buddhist mystics write about; but the truth is that he tried many experiments to do this and never succeeded. He did, however, discover that when ordinary senses get weaker, other ones can develop to make up for it; he became quite skilled at telepathy, and though he never claimed any special healing powers, there was something about just being near him that helped certain illnesses.

You might wonder how he spent his time during these unprecedented years. His attitude can be summed up by saying that since he hadn't died at a normal age, he began to feel there was no real reason why he should or shouldn't die at any particular time in the future. Having already proved himself unusual, it seemed just as easy to believe the unusualness might continue as to expect it to end suddenly. And since that was true, he started living without worrying about death as he had for so long; he began living the kind of life he had always wanted but rarely found possible—because at heart, through all his adventures, he had always had the peaceful tastes of a scholar.

His memory was amazing; it seemed to have escaped physical limits into some higher realm of perfect clarity. It almost seemed he could now learn everything more easily than he had been able to learn anything as a student. Of course, he soon ran into the problem of needing books, but he had a few with him from the beginning, including (you might be interested to know) an English grammar, a dictionary, and Florio's translation of Montaigne. Using these, he managed to master the complexities of your language, and we still have in our library his manuscript of one of his first language exercises—a translation of Montaigne's essay on Vanity into Tibetan—surely the only one of its kind ever made."

Conway smiled. "I'd love to see that sometime, if I might."

"With the greatest pleasure. It was, you might think, a rather impractical thing to do, but remember that Perrault had reached a rather impractical age. He would have been lonely without some such occupation—at least until the fourth year of the nineteenth century, which marks an important event in our history. For that's when a second stranger from Europe arrived in Blue Moon Valley.

He was a young Austrian named Henschell who had fought against Napoleon in Italy—a youth of noble birth, high culture, and great charm. The wars had ruined his fortune, and he had wandered across Russia into Asia with some vague idea of making it back. It would be interesting to know exactly how he reached the plateau, but he had no clear idea himself; indeed, he was as close to death when he arrived here as Perrault himself had once been. Again Shangri-La offered its hospitality, and the stranger recovered—but there the similarity ends. For Perrault had come to preach and convert, while Henschell was more immediately interested in the gold deposits. His first ambition was to get rich and return to Europe as soon as possible.

But he didn't return. An odd thing happened—though one that has happened so often since that perhaps we must now agree it isn't so odd after all. The valley, with its peacefulness and complete freedom from worldly worries, tempted him again and again to delay his departure, and one day, having heard the local legend, he climbed to Shangri-La and had his first meeting with Perrault.

That meeting was truly historic. Perrault, if perhaps beyond such human feelings as friendship or affection, still had a rich kindness of mind that touched the youth like water on parched soil. I won't try to describe the relationship that grew between them; one gave complete devotion, while the other shared his knowledge, his moments of joy, and the wild dream that had now become the only reality left for him in the world."

There was a pause, and Conway said very quietly: "Pardon the interruption, but that's not quite clear to me."

"I know." The whispered reply was completely understanding. "It would be remarkable if it were. It's something I'll be pleased to explain before our talk is over, but for now, if you'll forgive me, I'll stick to simpler things. One interesting fact is that Henschell started our collections of Chinese art, as well as our library and musical acquisitions. He made an amazing journey to Peking and brought back the first group of items in 1809. He never left the valley again, but it was his cleverness that created the complicated system by which the monastery has ever since been able to get anything it needs from the outside world."

"I suppose you found it easy to make payment in gold?"

"Yes, we've been fortunate to have supplies of something that's considered so valuable in other parts of the world."

"So valuable that you must have been very lucky to avoid a gold rush."

The High Lama made the smallest nod of agreement. "That, my dear Conway, was always Henschell's fear. He was careful that none of the porters bringing books and art treasures should ever come too close; he made them leave their loads a day's journey away, to be collected later by our valley people. He even arranged for guards to keep constant watch on the entrance to the pass. But soon he thought of an easier and more final solution."

"Yes?" Conway's voice was carefully controlled.

"You see, we never needed to fear invasion by an army. That will never be possible, given the nature and distances of the country. The most we could expect was the arrival of a few half-lost wanderers who, even if armed, would probably be too weak to be dangerous. So it was decided that from then on, strangers could come as freely as they wished—with just one important condition.

And over many years, such strangers did come. Chinese merchants, trying to cross the plateau, sometimes found this one path out of so many possible routes. Wandering Tibetan nomads sometimes strayed here like tired animals. All were welcomed, though some only reached the shelter of the valley to die. In 1815, two English missionaries traveling overland to Peking crossed the ranges by an unnamed pass and had the extraordinary luck to arrive as calmly as if making a social call. In 1820, a Greek trader and his sick, starving servants were found dying at the highest ridge of the pass. In 1822, three Spaniards, having heard a vague story about gold, reached here after many wanderings and disappointments. Then in 1830, there was a larger group. Two Germans, a Russian, an Englishman, and a Swede made the dreaded crossing of the Tian-Shan mountains, driven by what would become an increasingly common motive—scientific exploration.

By this time, Shangri-La had slightly changed its attitude toward visitors—not only were they welcomed if they happened to find their way into the valley, but it had become customary to meet them if they came within a certain distance. All this was for a reason I'll explain later, but it's important because it shows that the monastery was no longer just passively hospitable; it now both needed and wanted new arrivals. And indeed in the years that followed, more than one group of explorers, thrilled by their first distant glimpse of Karakal, met messengers carrying a friendly invitation—one that was rarely refused.

Meanwhile the monastery had begun to take on many of its present features. I must emphasize that Henschell was extremely capable and talented, and today's Shangri-La owes as much to him as to its founder. Yes, quite as much, I often think. For his was the firm but kind hand that every institution needs at a certain stage of its development, and losing him would have been completely devastating if he hadn't accomplished more than a lifetime's work before he died."

Conway looked up to echo rather than question those final words. "He died!"

"Yes. It was very sudden. He was killed. It happened in 1857. Just before his death, a Chinese artist had sketched him, and I can show you that sketch now—it's in this room."

The slight hand gesture was repeated, and once again a servant entered. Conway, as if watching a dream, saw the man pull back a small curtain at the far end of the room and leave a lantern swinging in the shadows. Then he heard the whisper inviting him to move, the whisper that had already become familiar music.

He got to his feet and walked over to the trembling circle of light.

The sketch was small, hardly bigger than a miniature in colored inks, but the artist had somehow made the flesh tones look as delicate as wax. The features were beautifully drawn, almost girlish, and Conway found them instantly appealing, even across the barriers of time, death, and art. But the strangest thing, which he only realized after his first gasp of admiration, was that the face was that of a young man.

He stammered as he moved away: "But—you said—this was done just before his death?"

"Yes. It's a very good likeness."

"Then if he died in the year you said—"

"He did."

"And he came here, you told me, in 1803, when he was a youth?"

"Yes."

Conway was quiet for a moment; finally, with effort, he asked: "And he was killed, you were saying?"

"Yes. An Englishman shot him. It was a few weeks after the Englishman had arrived at Shangri-La. He was another explorer."

"What caused it?"

"There had been an argument—about some porters. Henschell had just told him the important condition that governs our reception of guests. It was a difficult task, and ever since, despite my own weakness, I've felt I must do it myself."

The High Lama paused longer this time, with just a hint of question in his silence; when he continued, he added: "Perhaps you're wondering, my dear Conway, what that condition might be?"

Conway answered slowly and quietly: "I think I can already guess."

"Can you, indeed? And can you guess anything else after this long and curious story of mine?"

Conway felt dizzy as he tried to answer; the room was now a whirl of shadows with that ancient, kindly presence at its center. Throughout the story, he had listened so intently that it had perhaps protected him from realizing the full meaning of it all; now, just trying to put it into words, he was overwhelmed with amazement, and the growing certainty in his mind was almost choked as it came out. "It seems impossible," he stammered. "And yet I can't help thinking of it—it's astonishing—and extraordinary—and quite incredible—and yet not completely beyond my ability to believe—"

"What is, my son?"

And Conway answered, shaken with an emotion he didn't

understand and didn't try to hide: "That you are still alive, Father Perrault."

CHAPTER 8

There had been a pause while the High Lama asked for more tea. Conway didn't mind the break - he needed time to process everything he'd heard so far. While a servant prepared the tea in the traditional way, Conway thought about how surreal this all was: sitting in a heated room at the top of a hidden monastery, drinking tea with this mysterious man who seemed both ancient and somehow timeless.

The High Lama took a careful sip of the steaming tea before continuing his story. "Now I must tell you about something very important," he said in his soft, whispery voice. "You see, during those long weeks when Father Perrault was so close to death, he had a vision - an idea so powerful it changed everything about Shangri-La forever."

Conway leaned forward slightly, careful not to seem too eager. But the High Lama noticed anyway and gave a tiny smile.

"Perrault had been thinking deeply about the world," he continued. "He saw how people everywhere were becoming more violent, more focused on machines and weapons. He worried that all the beautiful things humans had created - art, music, books, ideas about kindness and wisdom - might be destroyed. And here was Shangri-La, peaceful and protected, where time itself seemed to move differently..."

"Differently?" Conway asked quietly, though he was starting to guess what the High Lama meant.

"Yes. You've noticed, haven't you? How Chang never gives clear answers about ages? How that young Manchu girl plays music that someone her age shouldn't even know about? How some of our books and art pieces seem impossibly old to be in such perfect condition?"

Conway nodded slowly. "I had noticed. But I didn't want to jump to conclusions."

"That's one of the things I like about you, Conway. You observe carefully but don't rush to judge what you see." The High Lama's eyes seemed to sparkle in the dim light. "The truth is, time works differently here in Shangri-La. People age much, much more slowly than they do anywhere else in the world."

Even though Conway had started to suspect something like this, hearing it said plainly still shocked him. "How is that possible?" he asked.

"It's partly the special air in our valley," the High Lama explained. "Partly the herbs that grow here. And partly something else - something we don't fully understand ourselves. But we know it works. Most people who come to live at Shangri-La can expect to live to be very, very old while staying healthy and clear-minded."

Conway thought about this. It explained so many things - why the monastery seemed to mix old and new so naturally, why everyone was so careful about telling time, why no one seemed eager to leave. Then a startling thought hit him.

"You..." he began carefully. "Are you...?"

The High Lama's smile grew slightly wider. "Yes, Conway. I am Father Perrault. The same person who first found this valley over two hundred years ago."

Conway sat very still, letting this sink in. The person sitting across from him had lived through the American Revolution, the French Revolution, Napoleon's wars, the Industrial Revolution, World War I... It was almost too much to take in.

"I've changed a great deal since then," the High Lama continued. "When you live as long as I have, your mind becomes different. Calmer. You start to see things from a greater distance, like looking down from a very high mountain."

"But why?" Conway asked. "Why create all this? Why bring people here?"

"Ah, now we come to the heart of it." The High Lama straightened slightly in his chair. "You see, Perrault - or I should say, I - realized that the world was heading toward disaster. People were creating more and more powerful weapons. Nations were becoming more aggressive. Another war was coming - perhaps even worse than the last one. And someone needed to protect humanity's greatest treasures: our art, our music, our books, our knowledge about how to live peacefully and wisely."

"So Shangri-La is like... a sanctuary?" Conway asked.

"Exactly! A place where the best things humans have created can be kept safe until the world is ready for them again. A place where people can live in peace and study and grow wiser. A place where time moves slowly enough for us to really learn and understand things."

"And that's why you brought us here?" Conway couldn't help asking. "Me and my companions?"

"Yes. We need new people at Shangri-La. People who can help preserve knowledge and wisdom. People who can appreciate beauty and understand why it's worth protecting." The High Lama paused. "Especially people like you, Conway."

"Me? Why me?"

"Because you have the right qualities. You're observant. You think carefully about things. You appreciate both Eastern and Western ways of thinking. And most importantly, you have what I call the gift of contentment - you know how to be happy with where you are instead of always rushing to be somewhere else."

Conway thought about this. It was true - even when they'd first arrived, part of him had felt strangely at home here. But then he thought about his companions.

"What about the others?" he asked. "Will you tell them all this too?"

The High Lama shook his head slowly. "Not yet. Some people need more time to accept such strange ideas. You were ready - I could tell from the way you've been since you arrived. The others may need longer to prepare themselves for the truth."

Conway nodded. He understood completely. Even he was having trouble fully accepting it all, and he was probably the most open-minded of the group. He could imagine how Mallinson would react, or Miss Brinklow...

"There's much more to tell you," the High Lama said. "Much more to explain about how we live here, how we get the things we need, how we choose new people to join us. But I'm tired now, and you need time to think about what you've learned. We'll talk again soon."

As Conway left the room that night, his head was spinning with everything he'd discovered. Shangri-La wasn't just a hidden monastery - it was a shelter for civilization itself, trying to preserve humanity's greatest achievements against the storms of history. And somehow, impossibly, he was now part of its story.

He walked out onto one of the terraces and looked up at the moonlit peak of Karakal. It looked different now that he knew the truth. Everything about Shangri-La looked different. He wasn't just seeing a beautiful place anymore - he was seeing a miracle.

The cold mountain air helped clear his head. He thought about everything the High Lama had told him, trying to make sense of it all. Part of him still wanted to doubt, to say it was impossible. But another part - the part that had felt strangely at home here from the beginning - knew it was true.

He thought about what the High Lama had said about another war coming. Conway had fought in the last one; he knew how horrible war could be. If Shangri-La could really preserve the best parts of human civilization while the world tore itself apart... well, maybe that was worth believing in impossible things for.

In the distance, he could hear the faint sound of music floating up from somewhere in the monastery - probably the Manchu girl practicing on the harpsichord. The familiar melody seemed different now too, knowing it was being played by someone who might have learned it hundreds of years ago.

Conway smiled to himself. He had so many questions still: How exactly did the slowing of time work? How did they choose who to bring here? What would happen to him and his companions now? But those were questions for another day. For now, he was content just knowing he was part of something extraordinary - something that stretched back centuries into the past and might continue centuries into the future.

As he headed back to his room, he thought about how differently his three companions might take this news when they eventually learned it. Miss Brinklow would probably want scientific proof. Mallinson would likely be horrified at the idea of staying here forever. And Barnard... well, Barnard might actually like it, now that Conway thought about it. A place where no one from the outside world could ever find him? That might sound pretty good to a man on the run.

When Conway returned to his room that night, his mind was too active to sleep right away. He sat by his window, looking out at the moonlit valley, and remembered something else the High Lama had said earlier.

"You might wonder," he had whispered, "why I chose to tell you all this tonight. Why not wait longer? But you see, my dear Conway, I don't have much time left."

Conway had looked at him sharply. "But I thought you said—"

"Even here, death comes eventually," the High Lama had explained gently. "We don't stop time completely; we just slow it down. And after two hundred years, I can feel my time drawing to a close. That's why I need you to understand everything now."

"What do you mean?"

"Someone will need to take my place when I'm gone. Someone with wisdom, patience, and understanding. Someone who can guide Shangri-La into the future."

Conway had felt a chill run through him. "Surely you don't mean —"

"We'll talk more about that later," the High Lama had said with a small smile. "For now, just think about what you've learned. Watch. Observe. Try to understand what Shangri-La truly is."

Now, sitting in his room, Conway thought he was beginning to understand. Shangri-La wasn't just a place that preserved old things - it was a place that preserved old wisdom, ancient ways of thinking and seeing the world. In the outside world, everything moved so fast. People rushed from place to place, always wanting more, always fighting for more. But here, in this hidden valley, people had the time to think deeply about things, to appreciate beauty, to find real happiness.

He thought about his own life - all the running around he'd done, all the diplomatic missions and political crises he'd dealt with. Had any of it really mattered? Had it made him or anyone else truly happy? Here at Shangri-La, even after just a few weeks, he felt more peaceful than he had in years.

But what about his duty to the outside world? What about his job, his responsibilities? Conway had always been good at seeing both sides of things, but this was the biggest decision he'd ever faced. Stay here forever in this peaceful paradise, or return to the rushed and troubled world he came from?

The sound of wind whistling around the monastery brought another thought: maybe he didn't have to decide right away. After all, they couldn't leave until spring anyway - the mountain passes would be completely blocked by snow during winter. He had months to think about it, to learn more, to understand better.

He got up from his window and finally got ready for bed. Tomorrow would bring new questions, new discoveries. But for now, he felt strangely at peace. Whatever happened, he had learned something extraordinary - not just about Shangri-La, but about what was possible in the world. Some things that seemed impossible could be true after all.

As he drifted off to sleep, Conway thought he heard the faint sound of music again - not the harpsichord this time, but something else, something older. Maybe it was just his imagination, or maybe it was the monks chanting in their hidden rooms. Either way, it sounded like the voice of Shangri-La itself, ancient and peaceful, whispering secrets that had waited centuries to be heard.

CHAPTER 9

When Conway woke up the next morning, everything felt like a dream. Had his conversation with the High Lama really happened? It seemed too incredible to be true.

But he didn't have much time to wonder about it. As soon as he walked into breakfast, his companions bombarded him with questions.

"You sure had a long talk with the boss last night," Barnard said. "We tried to wait up for you, but got too tired. What's he like?"

"Did he say anything about getting us porters?" Mallinson asked eagerly.

"I hope you mentioned my idea about having a missionary here," Miss Brinklow added.

Conway felt himself putting up his usual defensive walls. It was strange - he already felt protective of Shangri-La's secrets, even though he'd only learned them hours ago. "I'm afraid I'm going to disappoint you all," he said carefully. "I didn't discuss missions with him. He didn't mention anything about porters. And as for what he's like - well, he's a very old man who speaks excellent English and seems quite intelligent."

"The main thing we care about," Mallinson cut in impatiently, "is whether we can trust him or not. Do you think he's planning to trick us somehow?"

"He didn't strike me as dishonest," Conway replied.

"Then why didn't you ask him about the porters?" Mallinson demanded. "That's the most important thing!"

"It didn't occur to me."

Mallinson stared at him like he couldn't believe his ears. "I don't understand you anymore, Conway. You were so amazing during that crisis in Baskul - you saved everyone! But now you seem like a completely different person. It's like you don't even care what happens to us."

"I'm sorry."

"Being sorry doesn't help! You need to pull yourself together and act like you care!"

"I meant I was sorry to disappoint you," Conway said quietly.

His voice was calm, but inside his feelings were all mixed up. He was surprised at how easily he could avoid telling the truth, but he knew he had to keep the High Lama's secret. He also felt bad about disappointing Mallinson, who had always looked up to him so much. It reminded him of how students at school sometimes hero-worship their sports captains, and how sad they feel when their heroes turn out to be just normal people.

But Conway couldn't pretend to be something he wasn't - not here. There was something about the air in Shangri-La that made fake emotions impossible. Maybe it was the high altitude, or maybe it was just the peaceful atmosphere of the place.

"Look, Mallinson," he said, "it's no use comparing this to what happened in Baskul. That was completely different."

"Yeah, and much healthier!" Mallinson shot back. "At least then we knew what we were dealing with."

"Murder and riots," Conway reminded him. "You can call that healthier if you want to."

"Well, I do!" Mallinson's voice got higher with frustration. "I'd rather face something I can see than all this mystery. Like that Chinese girl - how did she get here? Did he tell you that?"

"No. Why should he?"

"Well, why shouldn't he? And why didn't you ask? Isn't it weird to find a young girl living in a monastery full of monks?"

Conway hadn't thought about it that way before. "This isn't an ordinary monastery," was all he could think to say.

"You can say that again!"

They all fell silent. Miss Brinklow looked up from the Tibetan grammar book she was studying (as if, Conway thought with hidden amusement, she didn't have the rest of her life to learn it). "The morals of this place are absolutely terrible," she said firmly. She turned to Barnard for support, but the American just grinned.

"I don't think you folks want my opinion about morals," he said. "But I will say that fighting with each other is just as bad. Since we're stuck here for a while, we might as well try to get along and make ourselves comfortable."

Conway thought this was good advice, but Mallinson wasn't finished. "I bet you do find it more comfortable than prison," he said meanly to Barnard.

"Prison? Oh, you mean Dartmoor!" Barnard laughed. "Well, yes, this is definitely nicer than jail. And you know what? It doesn't hurt my feelings when you bring that up. I'm thick-skinned but tender-hearted - that's just how I am."

Conway looked at Barnard with new respect, and gave Mallinson a disapproving glance. But suddenly he felt like they were all actors in a play, and he was the only one who knew what the play was really about. That knowledge, which he couldn't share, made him want to be alone.

He nodded to the others and walked out into the courtyard. As soon as he saw the great mountain peak of Karakal, his worries faded away. His companions' complaints seemed so small compared to the amazing truth about Shangri-La. He realized that when everything around you is strange enough, you stop being surprised by anything. He'd felt something similar during the war - after a while, even the most shocking things started to seem normal.

He knew he would need that calmness to live his double life. With his fellow travelers, he had to pretend he was just waiting for porters to take them back to India. But the rest of the time, he could see a much bigger picture - one where time moved differently and the name "Blue Moon" had a special meaning, as if this amazing future could only happen once in a blue moon.

Sometimes he wondered which of his two lives felt more real, but he didn't worry about it too much. It reminded him again of the war, when during heavy bombing he would feel like he had many lives, and death could only take one of them.

Chang now talked to him completely openly, and they had many conversations about life in the monastery. Conway learned that during his first five years, he would live normally, without any special rules. "This is always done," Chang explained, "to let the body get used to the altitude, and to give time for getting over any sadness about the past."

Conway smiled. "So you're sure that no feeling of love or friendship can last longer than five years?"

"Oh, it can," Chang replied, "but only as a gentle memory that makes us a little sad in a pleasant way."

After those first five years, Chang explained, they would start the process of slowing down aging. If it worked, Conway might be able to stay looking about forty years old for another fifty years or so.

"What about you?" Conway asked. "How did it work for you?"

"Ah, I was very lucky," Chang said. "I came here when I was quite young - only twenty-two. I was a soldier, if you can believe it! I was leading troops against bandits in 1855. I got lost in the mountains with my men - only seven out of a hundred survived the terrible weather. When I was finally rescued and brought to Shangri-La, I was so sick that only being young and strong saved me."

"Twenty-two," Conway said thoughtfully, doing the math in his head. "So you're ninety-seven now?"

"Yes. Very soon, if the lamas agree, I'll become a full member of their order."

"I see. You have to wait for a round number?"

"No, there's no strict age limit, but we usually think that by a hundred years old, people have moved past the strong emotions of regular life."

"That makes sense. And what happens after that? How long do you expect to live?"

"We hope I'll have the same advantages Shangri-La gives to all its lamas - perhaps another century or more."

Conway nodded. "I don't know whether to congratulate you - you seem to have the best of both worlds. A long, happy youth behind you, and an equally long, peaceful old age ahead. When did you start looking older?"

"When I was past seventy. That's pretty common, though I think I still look younger than my actual age."

"Definitely. And what would happen if you left the valley now?"

"I would die if I stayed away more than a few days."

"So the air here is essential?"

"There is only one Blue Moon Valley," Chang said, "and anyone who expects to find another is asking too much of nature."

"Well, what would have happened if you'd left thirty years ago, during your extended youth?"

"I probably would have died even then," Chang answered. "At the very least, I would have quickly started looking my real age. We had an interesting example of that a few years ago - though it wasn't the first time. One of our people, a Russian, left the valley to look for some travelers we'd heard might be coming. He was almost eighty but looked about forty. He was only supposed to be gone a week, which would have been fine, but some nomads captured him and took him away. After three months, he managed to escape and return to us. But he was completely changed - he looked every one of his eighty years, and he died soon after, like any old man would."

Conway was quiet for a while. They were talking in the library, and he found himself staring through a window at the mountain pass that led to the outside world. A small wisp of cloud floated past the ridge. "That's a pretty grim story, Chang," he finally said. "It makes Time feel like some angry monster waiting outside the valley, ready to attack anyone who's managed to escape it for too long."

"Monster?" Chang asked, confused by the English word.

"In this case, I meant a frightening creature," Conway explained. "But I wasn't being entirely serious."

Chang bowed in thanks for the explanation. He loved learning about languages and liked to think carefully about new words. "It's interesting," he said after a pause, "that English people think being lazy is bad. We would much rather be lazy than tense. Isn't there too much tension in the world right now? Wouldn't it be better if more people were lazy?"

"I think you might be right about that," Conway answered with an amused smile.

Over the next week or so, Conway met several other lamas. Chang didn't rush to introduce him but didn't avoid it either. There was a nice atmosphere where nothing felt urgent but nothing felt disappointing either. "Some of the lamas might not meet you for years," Chang explained, "but don't worry about that. They're happy to meet you whenever it happens, and the fact that they don't rush doesn't mean they don't want to."

Conway, who often felt the same way about meeting new people himself, completely understood.

The meetings he did have went very well. He found it easy to talk to these men who were three times his age - easier than it would have been in London or Delhi. His first meeting was with a friendly German named Meister, who had come to the monastery in the 1880s after his exploring party got lost. He spoke good English, though with an accent. A few days later, Conway met someone the High Lama had specifically mentioned - Alphonse Briac, a small, energetic Frenchman who didn't look particularly old but said he had been a student of the famous composer Chopin. Conway thought both men would make good company.

After a few more meetings, Conway started noticing some patterns. Though each lama was different, they all had that quality he could only think to call "agelessness." They were all extremely intelligent in a calm way, and their opinions were always carefully thought out. Conway found it easy to talk with them, and they seemed to appreciate that about him. They were just as easy to get along with as any other group of educated people he might have met, though it was sometimes strange to hear them talk so casually about things that had happened so long ago.

For instance, one kind-looking man with white hair asked Conway if he was interested in the Brontë sisters. When Conway said yes, the man said, "You see, when I was a young priest in Yorkshire during the 1840s, I once visited their house and stayed with them. Since coming here, I've made a study of their whole story - I'm writing a book about it. Perhaps you'd like to look it over with me sometime?"

Conway said he'd like that, and later asked Chang about how clearly the lamas seemed to remember their past lives. Chang explained that it was part of their training. "One of the first steps in clearing your mind," he said, "is to see your whole past life like a big picture. When you've been here long enough, your old life will come into focus like you're adjusting a telescope. Everything will stand clear and still, with the right size and importance. Take your new friend, for instance - he now understands that the most important moment of his entire life was when he was a young man visiting that house where an old minister lived with his three daughters."

"So I suppose I'll have to start remembering my own important moments?" Conway asked.

"It won't be hard," Chang said. "They'll come to you on their own."

"I'm not sure I want them to," Conway answered thoughtfully.

But whatever his past might show him, Conway was finding happiness in the present. When he sat reading in the library or playing Mozart in the music room, he often felt a deep spiritual feeling, as if Shangri-La were actually alive - like it had caught all the magic of history and somehow kept it safe from time and death. At these moments, he often thought about his talk with the High Lama. He felt like there was a calm intelligence watching kindly over everything they did, silently reassuring them that all was well.

He would listen while Lo-Tsen played complicated music pieces and wonder what was behind her faint, impersonal smile that made her look like a flower just starting to open. She rarely spoke, even though she now knew Conway could speak her language. To Mallinson, who sometimes came to the music room, she hardly spoke at all. But Conway found something special in her silences.

Once he asked Chang about her history and learned that she came from a royal Chinese family. "She was supposed to marry a prince from Turkestan," Chang explained, "and was traveling to meet him when her carriers got lost in the mountains. They all would have died if our people hadn't found them."

"When did this happen?" Conway asked.

"In 1884. She was eighteen."

"Eighteen then?"

Chang nodded. "Yes, she's doing very well here, as you can see. She's made excellent progress."

"How did she react when she first arrived?"

"She was perhaps a little more unhappy about it than most - she didn't complain, but we could tell she was troubled for a while. It was unusual, of course - to stop a young girl on her way to her wedding... We were all especially eager for her to be happy here." Chang smiled gently. "The excitement of love doesn't make it easy to accept such changes, though the first five years proved long enough."

"I suppose she was deeply in love with the man she was going to marry?"

"Oh no, she had never met him. It was the old custom, you see. Her excitement wasn't about any particular person."

Conway nodded, feeling a bit sad for Lo-Tsen. He imagined her as she must have been fifty years ago, sitting properly in her decorated chair as her carriers struggled through the mountains, her eyes searching the harsh, windy landscape that must have seemed so different from the gentle gardens she knew. "Poor child!" he thought, picturing such a delicate person trapped here through the years. But knowing her story made him appreciate her quietness and calmness even more. She was like a beautiful vase that caught and held a single ray of light.

He also enjoyed, though less intensely, when Briac talked to him about Chopin and played his famous melodies brilliantly. It turned out that Briac knew several Chopin pieces that had never been published, and since he had written them down, Conway spent pleasant hours learning them himself. He found it exciting to think that none of the world's most famous pianists had ever played these pieces. Even better, Briac kept remembering little bits of music that Chopin had made up or played casually on various occasions. He wrote them all down as he remembered them, and some were very beautiful.

"Briac," Chang explained, "hasn't been a full lama very long, so you must forgive him if he talks about Chopin a lot. The younger lamas naturally think about the past a lot - it's a necessary step before they can start thinking about the future."

"Which is what the older ones do, I suppose?" Conway asked.

"Yes. The High Lama, for instance, spends almost all his time in deep meditation, seeing visions of what's to come."

Conway thought for a moment and then asked, "By the way, when do you think I'll see him again?"

"Probably at the end of your first five years," Chang said confidently.

But Chang was wrong about that, because less than a month after Conway arrived at Shangri-La, he received another invitation to visit the High Lama's hot, high room. Chang had told him that the High Lama never left his apartments and needed the heat to stay alive. Conway, knowing what to expect this time, found the heat less uncomfortable than before. He could breathe easily from the moment he bowed and saw that tiny spark of life in the High Lama's sunken eyes. He felt connected to the mind behind those eyes, and even though he knew this second meeting so soon after the first was a special honor, he wasn't nervous at all. Age didn't matter much to Conway - he never had trouble liking people just because they were too young or too old. He deeply respected the High Lama, but he didn't see why they couldn't have a friendly conversation.

They exchanged polite greetings, and Conway answered several questions. He said he was enjoying life at Shangri-La and had already made some friends.

"And have you kept our secrets from your three companions?" the High Lama asked.

"Yes, so far. It's been awkward sometimes, but probably less awkward than if I had told them."

"Just as I thought - you handled it well. And the awkwardness won't last forever. Chang tells me he thinks two of them won't give us much trouble."

"I think that's probably true."

"And the third?"

Conway replied, "Mallinson is a bit high-strung - he's very eager to leave."

"You like him?"

"Yes, I like him very much."

Just then servants brought in tea, and the conversation became lighter as they sipped the fragrant drink. It was a nice custom that let them move from serious topics to more casual chat. The High Lama asked Conway if he'd ever seen anywhere like Shangri-La in the Western world.

Conway smiled. "Well, yes, actually. It reminds me a bit of

Oxford, where I used to teach. The scenery isn't as good there, but they often study things that are just as impractical, and though even the oldest professors aren't nearly as old as you, they do seem to age in a similar way."

"You have a sense of humor, my dear Conway," the High Lama replied with a twinkle in his eye, "which we'll all be very grateful for in the years to come."

Conway liked how the High Lama could move easily between deep, serious topics and lighter conversation. It made him feel even more certain that coming to Shangri-La hadn't been an accident. Here was a place where time moved differently, where people could live for centuries while keeping both their wisdom and their ability to smile at life's little jokes.

He thought about his companions - Miss Brinklow with her determination to convert everyone, Barnard with his cheerful acceptance of their situation, and young Mallinson with his desperate desire to leave. They each saw Shangri-La so differently. But Conway was starting to see it as something bigger than any of them had imagined a place where the best parts of human nature could be preserved and protected, where wisdom could grow as slowly and naturally as the flowers in the valley below.

As he left the High Lama's room that day, Conway felt more certain than ever that he had found something incredibly rare - not just a hiding place, but a place where time itself had found a hiding place. And somehow, impossibly but wonderfully, he was now part of its story.

CHAPTER 10

"Extraordinary!" Chang said when he heard that Conway had seen the High Lama again. Coming from someone who rarely used strong words, this meant a lot. Chang explained that in all the history of Shangri-La, no new arrival had ever been invited to see the High Lama twice before spending their first five years at the monastery. "You see," he explained, "it's very tiring for him to talk to newcomers. Their emotions and passions are usually too strong and unsettling for someone his age. Though I'm sure he knows what he's doing. Perhaps it teaches us all an important lesson - that even the fixed rules of our community aren't completely fixed."

To Conway, of course, it didn't seem any more extraordinary than anything else about Shangri-La. After his third and fourth visits with the High Lama, it started feeling quite natural. The two of them seemed to understand each other perfectly - when Conway was with the High Lama, all his usual worries and tensions just melted away, leaving him feeling completely peaceful. Sometimes he felt almost enchanted by the High Lama's incredible wisdom, but then they would share tea and talk about smaller things, and it felt like watching a complicated math problem turn into a beautiful poem.

Their conversations covered everything imaginable. They talked about philosophy, history, art, and music. The High Lama seemed to know everything about everything, but he never made Conway feel stupid or ignorant. Instead, Conway found himself thinking more deeply than he ever had before. Once, when he made a particularly good point in their discussion, the High Lama said, "My son, you're young in years, but I can see that your wisdom is much older. Surely something unusual must have happened to make you this way?"

Conway smiled. "Nothing more unusual than what happened to many others of my generation."

"I've never met anyone quite like you before."

Conway thought for a moment before answering. "There's no real mystery about it. The part of me that seems old to you got worn out by experiencing too much too young. From ages nineteen to twenty-two, I learned more than anyone should have to learn that quickly."

"You mean during the War?"

"Yes. Though I wasn't particularly unhappy then. I was excited and reckless and scared and angry. Like millions of other young men. I did terrible things and sometimes wonderful things. But it used up all my emotions too fast, and afterward everything felt boring and irritating. That's what made the years since then so hard. Though I've been pretty lucky overall."

"And so your education continued?"

Conway shrugged. "Maybe being tired of strong emotions is the beginning of wisdom, if you want to look at it that way."

"That," said the High Lama with a gentle smile, "is exactly what we believe at Shangri-La."

"I know. That's why I feel so at home here."

It was true. As days and weeks passed, Conway felt more and more content in both mind and body. Like Perrault and Henschell and the others before him, he was falling under Shangri-La's spell. The Blue Moon had captured him, and he didn't want to escape. The mountains gleamed around the valley like a wall of pure white, too bright to look at, and when he heard the harpsichord playing across the lotus pool, he felt like the music was weaving everything together into a perfect pattern of sight and sound.

He also realized, very quietly, that he was falling in love with Lo-Tsen, the Manchu girl. But it was a strange kind of love that didn't want or need anything in return. He appreciated her the way you might appreciate a beautiful painting or a perfect flower. When she performed her formal courtesies or touched the keyboard with her delicate fingers, that was all the closeness he needed. Sometimes he would speak to her in a way that might have led to more conversation if she wanted, but her answers never broke through her quiet privacy, and he was glad about that. He had suddenly understood one part of what made Shangri-La special - he had Time, endless Time for anything he wanted to happen. In a year or ten years, there would still be Time. He loved that idea, and it made him happy.

Meanwhile, he still had to deal with his regular life - with Mallinson's impatience, Barnard's cheerfulness, and Miss Brinklow's determination to change everything. He knew he'd be glad when they all finally learned the truth about Shangri-La, and like Chang, he thought neither the American nor the missionary would find it too hard to accept. He even had to smile when Barnard said one day, "You know, Conway, I'm starting to think this wouldn't be a bad place to settle down. I thought I'd miss newspapers and movies, but I guess you can get used to anything."

"I guess you can," Conway agreed.

Later he learned that Chang had taken Barnard down to the valley for what the American called a "night out." When Mallinson heard about this, he was scornful. "Getting drunk, I suppose," he said to Conway, and to Barnard himself he added, "Of course it's none of my business, but you'll want to stay in shape for the journey. The porters are due in two weeks, and from what I hear, the trip back won't be easy."

Barnard nodded calmly. "I never thought it would be. But as for staying in shape, I'm probably healthier than I've been in years. I get exercise every day, I don't have any worries, and the places down in the valley don't let you overdo things. Moderation, you know - that's their motto here."

"Yes, I'm sure you've been having a moderately good time," Mallinson said sharply.

"Sure have!" Barnard answered cheerfully. "This place has something for everyone - some people like Chinese girls who play the piano, right?" He winked at Conway.

Conway didn't mind the teasing, but Mallinson blushed angrily.

"Well, at least we can still put people in jail when they steal other people's money," he snapped.

"Sure, if you can catch them," Barnard said with another grin.

Then he announced something surprising: he wasn't planning to leave with the porters. He would wait for the next group, or maybe the one after that, if the monks would let him stay. He said there wasn't much point rushing back just to get arrested.

"You mean you're not coming with us?" Mallinson asked.

"That's right. I've decided to stick around for a while. It's fine for you - you'll get a hero's welcome when you get home. All I'll get is handcuffs."

"In other words, you're just afraid to face the consequences?"

"Well, I never did like consequences anyway."

Mallinson said coldly, "I suppose it's your business. Nobody can stop you from staying here your whole life if you want to." But he looked around at the others for support. "What do you say, Conway?"

"I agree - everyone has different ideas about things."

Mallinson turned to Miss Brinklow, who suddenly put down her book and said, "Actually, I think I'll stay too."

"What?" they all said together.

She smiled her usual bright, stiff smile. "You see, I've been thinking about how we all got here, and there's only one explanation - Providence brought us here for a reason. Don't you think so, Mr. Conway?"

Conway might have found it hard to answer, but Miss Brinklow went on quickly: "Who am I to question God's will? I was sent here for a purpose, and I shall stay."

"Do you mean you're going to try to start a mission here?" Mallinson asked.

"Not just try - I fully intend to! I know exactly how to handle these people. I'll get my way, don't worry. There's no real strength in any of them."

"And you think they're going to let you?"

"Or maybe she's so strong-minded they can't stop her," Barnard put in with a chuckle. "Like I said - this place has something for everyone!"

"Yes, if you like being in prison," Mallinson snapped.

"Well, there's two ways to look at that," Barnard said thoughtfully. "Think of all the people in the world who'd give anything to get away from their troubles and be in a place like this, only they can't escape! So who's really in prison - us or them?"

"That's the kind of thing a caged monkey would say to make himself feel better," Mallinson shot back. He was still angry.

Later, he spoke to Conway alone. "That man still gets on my nerves," he said, pacing around the courtyard. "I'm actually glad he won't be coming back with us. And I didn't appreciate his jokes about the Chinese girl."

Conway put a friendly hand on Mallinson's arm. He was genuinely fond of the young man, and their weeks together had only made him like him more, even when Mallinson was being difficult. "I thought he was teasing me about her, not you," he said gently.

"No, he meant it for me. He knows I'm interested in her. I am, Conway. I can't figure out why she's here, or if she's really happy. If I could speak her language like you do, I'd ask her straight out."

"I doubt you'd get much of an answer. She doesn't talk much to anyone."

"I don't understand why you don't ask her more questions."

"I don't really like interrogating people."

He wished he could say more. Suddenly he felt both sad and amused - this enthusiastic young man was going to take things very hard. "I wouldn't worry too much about Lo-Tsen," he added. "She's perfectly happy."

Now that Barnard and Miss Brinklow had decided to stay, things seemed both better and worse to Conway. Better because it meant fewer people to deal with when the truth finally came out, but worse because it left him and Mallinson apparently on opposite sides. It was a strange situation, and Conway wasn't sure how to handle it.

Fortunately, he didn't have to do anything right away. Until the two months were up, nothing much could happen. Afterward there would be a crisis no matter how much he prepared for it. He did mention once to Chang, "I'm worried about young Mallinson. He's going to take things very badly when he finds out."

Chang nodded sympathetically. "Yes, it won't be easy to convince him that this is actually good fortune. But the difficulty won't last forever. In twenty years, he'll be completely reconciled to being here."

Conway thought this was looking a bit too far ahead. "I'm wondering," he said, "how we're going to tell him the truth. He's counting the days until the porters arrive, and if they don't come —"

"But they will come."

"Oh? I thought all your talk about them was just a nice story to let us down easily."

"Not at all. Although we don't believe in being too strict about things here at Shangri-La, we do try to be moderately truthful. What I told you about the porters was almost completely true. We are expecting them around the time I said."

"Then you'll have trouble stopping Mallinson from going with them."

"We would never try to stop him. He'll simply discover - probably by trying it himself - that the porters regretfully cannot take anyone back with them."

"I see. So that's how you do it. And what do you expect to happen then?"

"Then, after being disappointed, since he is young and optimistic, he will probably start hoping that the next group of porters, due in nine or ten months, will be more willing to help him. And if we are wise, we won't immediately discourage that hope."

Conway frowned. "I'm not so sure about that. I think he's more likely to try escaping on his own."

"Escape? Is that really the right word? After all, the mountain pass is open to anyone at any time. We don't have any guards except the ones Nature provided."

Conway smiled. "Well, you have to admit Nature did a pretty good job. But I don't suppose you rely on her completely. What about all those exploring parties that have found their way here? Was the pass always equally open when they wanted to leave?"

It was Chang's turn to smile. "Special situations sometimes require special solutions."

"I see. So you only give people a chance to escape when you know they'd be foolish to take it?"

"Well, it has happened occasionally that people leave, but usually they're glad to come back after spending one night on the high plateau."

"Without shelter or proper clothes - yes, I can understand that. Your gentle methods work just as well as harsh ones. But what about the unusual cases who don't come back?"

"As you said yourself," Chang replied, "they don't come back." But he quickly added, "However, I can assure you that very few have been so unfortunate, and I trust your friend won't be rash enough to join their number."

Conway wasn't completely reassured by this, and Mallinson's future remained a worry. He wished the young man could be allowed to return with permission, like Talu the pilot had. Chang admitted that the authorities could allow this if they wanted to. "But would we be wise," he asked, "to trust our whole future to your friend's feelings of gratitude?"

Conway had to admit this was a good point, because Mallinson had made it very clear what he would do as soon as he reached

India. It was his favorite topic of conversation.

But all of that belonged to the everyday world that was gradually being pushed out of Conway's mind by the rich, fascinating world of Shangri-La. Except when he worried about Mallinson, he was extraordinarily content. He kept discovering new things about this place that seemed perfectly suited to his own needs and interests.

Once he asked Chang, "By the way, how do you handle love here? I suppose sometimes people who come here develop romantic feelings?"

"Quite often," Chang replied with a broad smile. "The lamas themselves are beyond such things, of course, and so are most of us when we get older, but until then we're like other men - except that I think we behave more reasonably. And I should tell you, Mr. Conway, that Shangri-La's hospitality includes everything. Your friend Mr. Barnard has already taken advantage of that."

Conway returned the smile. "Thanks," he answered dryly, "but I'm not particularly interested in that kind of thing right now. I was more curious about the emotional side."

"You find it easy to separate the two? Could it be that you're falling in love with Lo-Tsen?"

Conway was surprised by the direct question, though he tried not to show it. "What makes you ask that?"

"Because it would be quite appropriate if you were - in

moderation, of course. Lo-Tsen wouldn't respond with any great passion - that's more than you could expect - but it would be a very pleasant experience. And I speak with some authority, because I was in love with her myself when I was much younger."

"Were you? And did she respond then?"

"Only by showing the most charming appreciation of the compliment I paid her, and by a friendship that has grown more precious over the years."

"In other words, she didn't respond?"

"If you prefer to put it that way." Chang added thoughtfully, "She has always been good at sparing her admirers from the disappointment that comes with getting everything they want."

Conway laughed. "That might work for you and me, but what about someone young and passionate like Mallinson?"

"My dear sir, it would be the best possible thing that could happen! Not for the first time would Lo-Tsen comfort someone who is sad about learning he can't leave."

"Comfort?"

"Yes, though you mustn't misunderstand what I mean. Lo-Tsen doesn't give physical affection, except for how her very presence touches troubled hearts. Shakespeare said of Cleopatra that 'she makes hungry where she most satisfies' - that kind of passionate woman would be completely out of place at Shangri-La. Lo-Tsen, if I might change the quote, removes hunger where she least satisfies. It's a more delicate and lasting achievement."

"And one she has lots of practice in performing?"

"Oh yes - we've had many examples of it. She has a way of calming desire into a pleasant murmur that doesn't mind being unanswered."

"So in that sense, you could consider her part of the training equipment of the establishment?"

"You could look at it that way if you wished," Chang replied smoothly. "But it would be more graceful, and just as true, to compare her to a rainbow reflected in a glass bowl, or to dewdrops on a fruit tree's blossoms."

"I completely agree with you, Chang. That would be much more graceful." Conway enjoyed these careful back-and-forth conversations that his friendly teasing of the Chinese often produced.

But the next time he was alone with Lo-Tsen, he realized Chang's comments had been very perceptive. There was something about her that touched his emotions, warming them without burning. And suddenly he understood that Shangri-La and Lo-Tsen were perfectly matched - both beautiful in a way that made you peaceful instead of excited. For years his feelings had been like a sore nerve that the world kept bumping against, but now at last the pain was gone. He could feel love that wasn't torment or boredom. Sometimes when he walked past the lotus pool at night, he imagined holding her, but the sense of endless time washed over the thought, leaving him content just to wait and dream.

He didn't think he had ever been so happy, not even before the War had changed everything. He loved the peaceful world that Shangri-La offered, guided by its one great idea but not ruled by it. He loved how feelings here were wrapped in thoughts, and thoughts made gentler by the way they were expressed. Conway, who knew from experience that being rude didn't prove you were honest, also knew that speaking beautifully didn't mean you were lying. He loved the polite, unhurried atmosphere where conversation was an art, not just a habit. And he loved knowing that even the smallest things could now be enjoyed without worrying about wasting time, and the most delicate dreams could be welcomed into his mind.

Though Conway didn't meet any more of the lamas, he gradually learned more about what they did. Besides knowing many languages, some of them were doing research that would have amazed the outside world. Many were writing books; one was doing important work in mathematics; another was combining the ideas of two great historians to write a complete history of European civilization. But not all of them did such serious work, nor did any of them work all the time. Sometimes they just followed their interests wherever they led - like Briac with his old music, or the English ex-priest with his new ideas about a famous novel. And some did even smaller things that seemed completely impractical.

Once when Conway mentioned this, the High Lama told him a story about a Chinese artist who lived over two thousand years ago. This artist spent many years carving tiny dragons, birds, and horses on a cherry pit. When he finished, he offered his work to a prince. The prince couldn't see anything special about it at first, but the artist told him to "build a wall with a window in it, and look at the cherry pit through the window at sunrise." The prince did this and then saw that the tiny carving was actually very beautiful.

"Isn't that a lovely story?" the High Lama asked. "And don't you think it teaches us something valuable?"

Conway agreed. He was glad to know that Shangri-La's peaceful purpose could include all sorts of odd and seemingly useless activities, because he had always liked such things himself. Looking back at his life, he saw it full of projects he'd never had time to finish, but now they all seemed possible, even in moments of laziness. It was wonderful to think about, and he wasn't surprised when Barnard told him that he too saw an interesting future at Shangri-La.

Conway was spending more and more time with the High Lama now, and during one of their evening talks, something very important happened. As usual, they had been talking about many things, and the High Lama had asked about Conway's three companions. Then, very simply, he said: "Because, my son, I am going to die."

Conway couldn't speak for a moment - it seemed such an extraordinary statement. Finally, the High Lama continued: "You're surprised? But surely we're all mortal - even at Shangri-La. I might still have a few moments left, or even a few years. All I'm saying is that I can now see the end coming. You're very kind to look so concerned, and I won't pretend that even at my age, there isn't a touch of sadness in thinking about death.

Fortunately, very little of me is left that can die physically, and as for the rest - well, all religions agree in being optimistic about what comes next. I'm quite content, but I must get used to a strange feeling during my remaining hours - I must realize that I have time for only one more thing. Can you guess what that is?"

Conway remained silent.

"It concerns you, my son."

"You do me great honor."

"I plan to do much more than that."

Conway bowed slightly but didn't speak, and after waiting a while, the High Lama went on: "You know that these frequent talks between us have been unusual. But it's our tradition - if I may use that word about a place that isn't enslaved by tradition - that we never let rules become too rigid. We do what seems right, guided a little by the past but more by our present wisdom and our vision of the future. And that's why I feel encouraged to do this final thing."

Conway was still silent.

"I place in your hands, my son, the heritage and future of Shangri-La."

The words echoed in the quiet room. All Conway could hear was his own heart beating like a drum. Then, between beats, came the High Lama's words:

"I have waited for you, my son, for quite a long time. I have sat in this room and seen many new faces, looked into their eyes and heard their voices, always hoping that someday I would find you. My fellow lamas have grown old and wise, but you who are still young in years are already as wise as they are. My friend, what I'm giving you isn't a difficult task, because our order knows only gentle bonds. To be kind and patient, to care for the treasures of the mind, to watch wisely and secretly while the storm rages outside - it will all be very pleasantly simple for you, and you will surely find great happiness."

Conway tried to reply but couldn't. Finally, after a bright flash of lightning lit up the shadows, he managed to say, "The storm... this storm you talk about..."

"It will be unlike anything the world has ever seen," the High Lama said. "There will be no safety in weapons, no help from governments, no answers from science. It will rage until every flower of civilization is trampled and all human achievements are leveled in vast chaos. This was my vision even before Napoleon was known to history, and I see it more clearly with each passing hour. Do you think I'm mistaken?"

Conway answered carefully: "No, I think you may be right. Something similar happened once before, and then we had the Dark Ages lasting five hundred years."

"The comparison isn't quite exact," the High Lama said. "Those Dark Ages weren't really completely dark - they were full of little flickering lights, and even if Europe had gone completely dark, there were other lights all across the world, from China to Peru, that could have rekindled the flame. But the Dark Ages that are coming will cover the whole world in a single shadow. There will be no escape and no sanctuary, except for places too secret to find or too humble to notice. And Shangri-La may hope to be both of these. The pilots carrying death to great cities will not pass our way, and if by chance they should, they might not think us worth bombing."

"And you think all this will happen in my lifetime?"

"I believe you will live through the storm. And afterward, through the long age of destruction, you may still live, growing older and wiser and more patient. You will preserve the fragrance of our history and add your own touch to it. You will welcome strangers and teach them our rule of age and wisdom. And one of these strangers, perhaps, will take your place when you are very old. Beyond that, my vision grows weak, but I see, very far away, a new world stirring in the ruins, reaching for its lost and legendary treasures. And they will all be here, my son, hidden behind the mountains in the valley of Blue Moon, preserved as if by miracle for a new Renaissance..."

The High Lama's voice faded away, and Conway saw his face full of a distant, overwhelming beauty. Then the glow faded and there was nothing left but a mask, shadowed and crumbling like old wood. It was completely still, and his eyes were closed. Conway watched for a while, and then, as if in a dream, he realized that the High Lama was dead.

He felt he needed to connect this moment to something real, or it might seem too strange to believe. Without thinking, he looked at his watch. It was 12:15. When he crossed the room to the door, he realized he had no idea how to get help or who to call. He knew all the Tibetan servants had been sent away for the night, and he didn't know where to find Chang or anyone else. He stood uncertainly at the door to the dark hallway. Through a window he could see that the sky was clear now, though lightning still played around the mountains like silver paint. And then, in the middle of what still felt like a dream, he suddenly knew that he was now master of Shangri-La.

All around him were the things he loved - the things that belonged to that inner world where he lived more and more, away from the world's troubles. His eyes wandered through the shadows and caught golden sparks dancing on rich, flowing lacquer work. The scent of tuberose flowers, so faint he could barely smell it, drew him from room to room. Finally he found himself in the courtyard by the lotus pool. A full moon sailed behind Karakal mountain. It was 1:40 in the morning.

Later, he became aware that Mallinson was beside him, holding his arm and trying to hurry him somewhere. He couldn't quite understand what was happening, but he could hear the boy chattering excitedly.

CHAPTER 11

Mallinson half-dragged Conway into the dining room, still holding his arm. "Hurry up, Conway! We have until dawn to pack what we need and get away. Great news - though I wonder what Barnard and Miss Brinklow will think in the morning when they find us gone... but it's their choice to stay, and we'll probably do better without them anyway... The porters are just over the pass - they arrived yesterday with loads of books and supplies... tomorrow they start their journey back... Just shows how these people here were planning to trick us - they never told us about the porters - we would have been stuck here forever..."

He stopped suddenly, noticing that Conway had slumped into a chair and was leaning forward with his head in his hands. "What's wrong? Are you sick?"

"No, not sick," Conway said, rubbing his eyes. "Just... very tired."

"Probably from the storm. Where were you all this time? I'd been waiting for hours."

"I was... visiting the High Lama."

"Oh, him! Well, that's the last time you'll have to do that, thank goodness."

"Yes, Mallinson. The last time."

Something in Conway's voice made Mallinson irritated. "Well, don't sound so calm about it - we need to hurry! We have a lot to do!"

Conway tried to focus. To test if he was really awake, he lit a cigarette. His hands were shaking. "I'm sorry," he said. "I don't quite understand... you said something about porters..."

"Yes, the porters! Come on, wake up!"

"You're thinking of going out to them?"

"Thinking about it? I'm absolutely certain! They're just over the ridge. And we have to leave right now."

"Right now?"

"Yes, yes - why not?"

Conway tried hard to pull himself from one world into another. Finally he said, "I suppose you realize this might not be as simple as it sounds?"

Mallinson was putting on thick Tibetan mountain boots as he answered impatiently: "I understand everything, but it's something we have to do, and we can do it if we don't waste time."

"I don't see how-"

"Oh come on, Conway! Have you lost all your courage? What's happened to you?"

The mix of anger and concern in Mallinson's voice helped Conway focus. "Whether I have or haven't isn't the point," he said. "But if you want me to explain, I will. There are some important details to consider. Even if you get over the pass and find the porters, how do you know they'll take you with them? What can you offer them? Haven't you thought they might not want to help? You can't just show up and demand they take you along. It needs planning, arrangements made ahead of time-"

"Or any other excuse to delay!" Mallinson interrupted bitterly. "What's happened to you? Thank goodness I don't have to depend on you for arrangements. Because they've already been made - the porters have been paid, and they've agreed to take us. And here are clothes and supplies for the journey, all ready. So you have no more excuses. Come on, let's go!"

"But... I don't understand..."

"I don't suppose you do, but it doesn't matter."

"Who arranged all this?"

Mallinson answered shortly: "Lo-Tsen, if you really want to

know. She's with the porters now. She's waiting."

"Waiting?"

"Yes. She's coming with us. I assume you don't mind?"

At the mention of Lo-Tsen, the two worlds Conway had been living in suddenly crashed together in his mind. "That's nonsense," he said sharply. "It's impossible."

"Why is it impossible?" Mallinson demanded.

"Because... well, it is. There are all kinds of reasons. Take my word for it - it won't work. I'm amazed she's even out there now, but the idea of her going any further is just ridiculous."

"I don't see why. It's just as natural for her to want to leave as it is for me."

"But she doesn't want to leave. That's where you're wrong."

Mallinson smiled tensely. "You probably think you know more about her than I do. But maybe you don't, even with all your languages."

"What do you mean?"

"There are other ways to understand people without knowing lots of languages."

"What are you talking about?" Conway took a deep breath. "This is silly. We shouldn't argue. Tell me, Mallinson, what's really going on? I still don't understand."

"Then why are you making such a big fuss?"

"Tell me the truth, please."

"Well, it's simple enough. A young girl her age, locked up here with all these strange old men - of course she wants to escape if she gets the chance. She's never had one before."

"Don't you think you might be seeing her situation through your own eyes? Like I've told you before, she's perfectly happy here."

"Then why did she say she'd come?"

"She said that? How could she? She doesn't speak English."

"I asked her - in Tibetan - Miss Brinklow helped me with the words. It wasn't a very good conversation, but it was enough to... to come to an understanding." Mallinson blushed slightly. "Come on, Conway, don't look at me like that - you'd think I was stealing something from you."

Conway answered quietly: "No one would think that, I hope, but what you just said tells me more than you meant it to. I can only say I'm very sorry."

"Sorry? Why should you be sorry?"

Conway dropped his cigarette. He felt tired and troubled, full of different kinds of caring that he wished hadn't been stirred up. He said gently: "I wish we weren't always misunderstanding each other. Lo-Tsen is very special, I know, but why should we fight about it?"

"Special?" Mallinson repeated scornfully. "She's much more than that. Don't think everyone's as cold about these things as you are. Maybe you're happy just admiring her like she's in a museum, but I actually try to help when I see someone I care about in a bad situation."

"But don't you think you might be rushing things? Where will she go if she leaves?"

"I suppose she must have friends in China or somewhere. Anyway, she'll be better off than here."

"How can you be so sure?"

"Well, I'll look after her myself if no one else will. After all, when you're rescuing someone from something horrible, you don't usually stop to ask if they have somewhere else to go."

"And you think Shangri-La is horrible?"

"Yes, I do. There's something dark and evil about it. Everything has been wrong from the start - the way we were brought here for no reason by some madman, and how we've been kept here with one excuse after another. But the worst thing - for me - is what it's done to you."

"To me?"

"Yes, to you. You've just wandered around like nothing matters, like you'd be happy to stay here forever. You even said you liked it... Conway, what's happened to you? Can't you be your real self again? We got along so well in Baskul - you were completely different then."

"My dear boy!"

Conway reached for Mallinson's hand, and Mallinson gripped back warmly. He went on: "You probably don't realize it, but I've been terribly lonely these past weeks. Nobody seemed to care about the only thing that really mattered - Barnard and Miss Brinklow had their own reasons for staying, but it was awful when I found out you were against me too."

"I'm sorry."

"You keep saying that, but it doesn't help."

Conway took a deep breath. "Then let me help by telling you something. When you hear it, you'll understand a lot of what seems strange and difficult now. At least you'll understand why Lo-Tsen can't possibly go back with you."

"I don't think anything could make me see that. And please make it quick, because we really need to go."

Then Conway told him everything - the whole story of Shangri-La as the High Lama had told it to him, with all the extra details he'd learned from Chang. It was the last thing he'd ever planned to do, but he felt that now it was necessary. Only one thing he kept back, because it was still too painful to talk about - the fact that the High Lama had died that night and chosen Conway to take his place.

He told the story clearly and easily, and as he spoke, he felt again the strange magic of that timeless world. Its beauty overwhelmed him as he described it, and often he felt like he was reading from a page in his memory, the words and ideas were so clear in his mind.

When he finished, he felt relieved. Surely this was the only solution. He looked up calmly, confident he had done the right thing.

But Mallinson just tapped his fingers on the table and said, after a long pause: "I really don't know what to say, Conway... except that you must be completely crazy..."

They stared at each other in silence - Conway disappointed and withdrawn, Mallinson fidgeting uncomfortably. "So you think I'm crazy?" Conway finally asked.

Mallinson gave a nervous laugh. "Well, what else can I think, after a story like that? I mean... really... it's just nonsense... there's nothing to argue about."

Conway looked and sounded very surprised. "You think it's nonsense?"

"Well... how else can I look at it? I'm sorry, Conway - it's a strong thing to say - but I don't see how any sane person could believe it."

"So you still think we were brought here by accident - by some crazy person who carefully planned to steal a plane and fly it a thousand miles just for fun?"

Conway offered another cigarette, and they both took one. The pause gave them both a moment to calm down. Then Mallinson said: "Look, there's no point arguing about details. Actually, your theory that these people sent someone out into the world to bring back strangers, and that this person deliberately learned to fly and waited until the right plane with the right number of passengers came along... well, I won't say it's completely impossible, though it does seem far-fetched. If that was all, we might consider it. But when you add all these other impossible things - all this about the lamas being hundreds of years old and having some magic potion for staying young... well, it just makes me wonder what's gotten into you."

Conway smiled. "Yes, I can see why it's hard to believe. Maybe I had trouble believing it at first too - I don't really remember. Of course it's an extraordinary story, but surely you've seen enough with your own eyes to know this is an extraordinary place. Think of everything we've actually seen - a hidden valley in unexplored mountains, a monastery with a library full of European books-"

"Oh yes, and central heating, and modern bathrooms, and afternoon tea, and everything else - it's all very amazing, I know."

"Well then, what do you make of it?"

"Not much, I admit. It's a complete mystery. But that's no reason to believe things that are physically impossible. Believing in hot baths because you've had them is different from believing in people hundreds of years old just because they tell you they are." He laughed nervously. "Look here, Conway, this place has gotten to you, and I don't blame you. Pack up and let's get out of here. We can finish this argument over dinner in London in a few months."

Conway answered quietly: "I have no desire to go back to that life at all."

"What life?"

"The life you're thinking of... dinners... parties... sports... all that..."

"But I didn't say anything about parties and sports! And what's wrong with them anyway? Do you mean you're not coming with me? You're going to stay here like the others? Then at least you won't stop me from getting out!" Mallinson jumped up with blazing eyes. "You're not thinking straight!" he cried.

"You're crazy, Conway, that's what's wrong with you! I know you're usually calm and I'm usually excited, but at least I'm sane! They warned me about you before I joined you at Baskul, and I thought they were wrong, but now I can see they weren't-"

"What did they warn you about?"

"They said you'd been shell-shocked in the War, and you'd been strange sometimes ever since. I'm not blaming you - I know it's not your fault - and I hate talking like this... Oh, I'll go. It's all terrible and sickening, but I must go. I gave my word."

"To Lo-Tsen?"

"Yes, if you want to know."

Conway held out his hand. "Goodbye, Mallinson."

"For the last time, you won't come?"

"I can't."

"Goodbye, then."

They shook hands, and Mallinson left.

Conway sat alone in the lantern-light. It seemed to him that all the most beautiful things were fragile and temporary, that the two worlds he lived in could never really come together, and that one of them was always hanging by a thread. After thinking for a while, he looked at his watch; it was ten minutes to three.

He was still at the table, smoking his last cigarette, when Mallinson came back. The young man burst in suddenly, and when he saw Conway, he stood in the shadows as if gathering his courage. He was silent until Conway asked, "What's happened? Why are you back?"

The naturalness of the question drew Mallinson forward. He pulled off his heavy sheepskin coat and sat down. His face was pale and his whole body was shaking. "I couldn't do it," he said, half sobbing. "That place where we had to use ropes - you remember? I got that far... but I couldn't manage it. I'm no good with heights, and in the moonlight it looked terrible. Pretty pathetic, isn't it?" He broke down completely until Conway calmed him. Then he added bitterly: "They don't need to worry about people getting in or out of here by land. But I wish I had an airplane full of bombs!"

"Why would you want that, Mallinson?"

"Because this place needs to be destroyed, whatever it is! It's unhealthy and wrong - and if your impossible story were true, it would be even worse! A bunch of withered old men waiting here like spiders for anyone who comes near... it's awful... who'd want to live to be that old anyway? And as for your precious High Lama, if he's half as old as you say he is, someone should put him out of his misery... Oh, why won't you come away with me, Conway? I hate begging you for my own sake, but I'm young and we've been good friends - doesn't my whole life mean anything to you compared to the lies of these terrible people? And Lo-Tsen - she's young too - doesn't she matter at all?"

"Lo-Tsen is not young," said Conway.

Mallinson looked up and began to laugh hysterically. "Oh no, not young at all, of course. She looks about seventeen, but I suppose you'll tell me she's really a well-preserved ninety."

"Mallinson, she came here in 1884."

"You're out of your mind!"

"Her beauty, Mallinson, like all beauty in the world, is fragile and needs people who understand its value. It's like an echo that can only live where gentle things are loved. Take her away from this valley and you'll see her fade like an echo dying away."

Mallinson laughed harshly. "I'm not afraid of that. She's only an echo here, if anywhere." After a pause, he added: "But this kind of talk isn't getting us anywhere. Let's be practical about this. Conway, I want to help you - I know it's all complete nonsense, but I'll discuss it if that will help. I'll pretend what you've told me is possible and really needs looking at. Now tell me seriously, what proof do you have for this story?"

Conway was silent.

"Just that someone told you an incredible tale. Even from someone you'd known and trusted all your life, you wouldn't believe that kind of thing without proof. And what proof do you have here? None at all, as far as I can see. Has Lo-Tsen ever told you her history?"

"No, but-"

"Then why believe it from someone else? And all this business about living forever - can you point to one real fact that supports it?"

Conway thought for a moment and mentioned the unknown Chopin pieces that Briac had played.

"Well, that means nothing to me - I'm not a musician. But even if they're real, couldn't he have gotten them some other way without his story being true?"

"Quite possible, I suppose."

"And then this method you say exists - of staying young and all that. What is it? You say it's some kind of drug - well, what drug? Have you ever seen it or tried it? Did anyone ever give you any actual facts about it?"

"Not in detail, I admit."

"And you never asked for details? It didn't strike you that such an amazing story needed any proof? You just believed it completely?" Pressing his advantage, he continued: "How much do you actually know about this place, apart from what you've been told? You've seen a few old men - that's all it comes down to. Beyond that, we can only say that the place is well-equipped and seems to be run on intellectual lines. We have no idea how or why it was built, and if they really want to keep us here, that's still a mystery, but surely all that's hardly a reason to believe any wild story that comes along! After all, you're usually so skeptical - you wouldn't believe everything you were told even in an English monastery - I really can't see why you should accept everything just because you're in Tibet!"

Conway nodded. Even in the middle of deeper thoughts, he had to admire a good argument. "That's a clever point, Mallinson. I suppose the truth is that when it comes to believing things without proof, we all tend to believe what we find most attractive."

"Well, I can't see anything attractive about living until you're half dead. I'd rather have a short life and an exciting one. And this talk about a future war - it all sounds pretty weak to me. How does anyone know when the next war will be or what it'll be like? Weren't all the experts wrong about the last war?" When Conway didn't reply, he added: "Anyway, I don't believe in saying things have to happen. And even if they did, there's no need to hide from them. Heaven knows I'd probably be terrified if I had to fight in a war, but I'd rather face it than bury myself here."

Conway smiled. "Mallinson, you have an amazing ability to misunderstand me. At Baskul you thought I was a hero - now you think I'm a coward. Actually, I'm neither - though of course it doesn't matter. When you get back to India, you can tell people, if you like, that I stayed in a Tibetan monastery because I was afraid of another war. It's not my reason at all, but I'm sure it'll be believed by the people who already think I'm crazy."

Mallinson answered sadly: "That's not fair. Whatever happens, I'd never say anything against you. You can count on that. I don't understand you - I admit that - but - but - I wish I did. Oh, I wish

I did. Conway, can't I help you somehow? Isn't there anything I can say or do?"

There was a long silence, which Conway finally broke by saying: "There's just one question I'd like to ask - if you'll forgive me for being very personal."

"Yes?"

"Are you in love with Lo-Tsen?"

The young man's pale face turned red. "I suppose I am. I know you'll say it's ridiculous and impossible, and maybe it is, but I can't help how I feel."

"I don't think it's ridiculous at all."

The argument seemed to have found a peaceful harbor after all its storms, and Conway added: "I can't help my feelings either. You and that girl happen to be the two people in the world I care most about... though you might think that's strange." He got up suddenly and walked around the room. "We've said all we can say, haven't we?"

"Yes, I suppose we have." But Mallinson went on in a sudden rush: "Oh, what stupid nonsense all this is - about her not being young! And horrible, disgusting nonsense too. Conway, you can't believe it! It's just too ridiculous. How can it mean anything real?"

"How can you know for sure that she is young?"

Mallinson turned away, his face showing a serious kind of shyness. "Because I do know... Maybe you'll think less of me for it... but I do know. I'm afraid you never really understood her, Conway. She seemed cold on the outside, but that was because of living here - it had frozen all her warmth. But the warmth was there."

"Waiting to be thawed?"

"Yes... you could say that."

"And she's young, Mallinson - you're completely sure of that?"

Mallinson answered softly: "Yes - she's just a girl. I felt so sorry for her, and we were both drawn to each other, I suppose. I don't think it's anything to be ashamed of. In fact, in a place like this, I think it's probably the most decent thing that's ever happened..."

Conway walked to the balcony and looked at the bright peak of Karakal; the moon was high in a smooth ocean of sky. He realized that a dream was dissolving, like all too beautiful things, at the first touch of reality; that all the world's future, weighed against youth and love, would be as light as air. And he knew that his mind lived in its own world, a miniature Shangri-La, and that this world too was in danger. Even as he tried to strengthen himself, he could feel his imagined world twisting and straining under the impact; the pavilions were falling; everything was about to collapse. He was only partly unhappy, but he was infinitely and sadly confused. He didn't know whether he had been sane and was now going mad, or had been mad and was now becoming sane again.

When he turned around, there was a change in him; his voice was sharper, almost rough, and his face twitched slightly; he looked much more like the Conway who had been a hero at Baskul. Ready for action, he faced Mallinson with sudden alertness. "Do you think you could manage that difficult bit with the rope if I were with you?" he asked.

Mallinson jumped forward. "Conway!" he cried chokingly. "You mean you'll come? You've finally decided?"

They left as soon as Conway had gathered what he needed for the journey. It was surprisingly easy to leave - more like a departure than an escape; they met no one as they crossed the patches of moonlight and shadow in the courtyards. Conway thought the monastery seemed completely empty; and immediately that feeling of emptiness became an emptiness inside him, while all the time, though he barely heard him, Mallinson was chattering excitedly about their journey.

How strange that their long argument should end like this in action, that this secret sanctuary should be left behind by someone who had found such happiness in it! For indeed, less than an hour later, they stopped to catch their breath at a bend in the path and saw Shangri-La for the last time. Far below them the Valley of Blue Moon was like a cloud, and to Conway the scattered roofs seemed to be floating after him through the mist. Now was the moment to say goodbye. Mallinson, who had been quiet while climbing the steep path, gasped out: "Good man, we're doing fine - keep going!"

Conway smiled but didn't answer; he was already getting the rope ready for the dangerous knife-edge traverse. It was true, as Mallinson had said, that he had made up his mind; but it was only what was left of his mind. That small, active part now controlled everything; the rest was just an emptiness he could hardly bear. He was a wanderer between two worlds and would always be wandering; but for now, in a deepening inner void, all he knew was that he liked Mallinson and had to help him; he was destined, like millions of others, to run away from wisdom and be a hero.

Mallinson was nervous at the dangerous cliff, but Conway helped him across using proper mountain-climbing techniques. When they were safely over, they rested and shared Mallinson's cigarettes. "Conway, I must say this is incredibly kind of you... I think you know how I feel... I can't tell you how glad I am..."

"Better not try, then," Conway said.

After a long pause, before they started walking again, Mallinson added: "But I am glad - not just for myself, but for you too... It's wonderful that you can finally see that all that stuff was complete nonsense... it's just great to see you being your real self again..."

"Not at all," Conway replied with a secret sadness.

Around dawn they crossed the highest point of the pass. No guards challenged them, though Conway wondered if maybe that was part of Shangri-La's way - to watch the path just carefully enough. Soon they reached the high plateau, swept clean as a bone by fierce winds, and after walking downhill for a while, they saw the porters' camp. Everything happened just as Mallinson had said - they found the men ready to go, strong fellows wrapped in furs and sheepskins, huddled against the wind and eager to begin their journey to Tatsien-Fu - eleven hundred miles east, on the Chinese border.

"He's coming with us!" Mallinson called out excitedly when they met Lo-Tsen. He forgot she didn't speak English, but Conway translated.

It seemed to Conway that the little Manchu had never looked so beautiful. She gave him a lovely smile, but her eyes were only for Mallinson.

And so they began their journey away from Shangri-La, though part of Conway knew that no journey would ever really take him away from it completely. In choosing to help his young friend, he had chosen to leave paradise - but perhaps that too was part of the High Lama's wisdom, that sometimes the noblest thing is not to keep wisdom for yourself, but to let it go for the sake of love.

EPILOGUE

I met Rutherford again in Delhi. We had been guests at a Viceregal dinner party, but with all the formalities and ceremonies, we barely spoke until afterward, when he invited me back to his hotel for a drink.

We shared a cab through the evening streets, past the grand government buildings of New Delhi and into the warm, lively maze of the old city. I knew from the newspapers that he had just returned from Kashgar. Rutherford had one of those carefully managed reputations that got the most out of everything; any unusual journey became an exploration in the public eye, and though he was careful never to do anything truly original, people didn't realize this and gave him full credit for his quick impressions. His latest journey into Tibet, as reported in the press, hadn't struck me as particularly remarkable—the buried cities of Khotan were old news to anyone who remembered Stein and Sven Hedin. When I mentioned this teasingly, he laughed. "Yes, the truth would have made a better story," he admitted with a mysterious smile.

In his hotel room, as we sat with our drinks, I finally asked what I'd been wondering: "So you did search for Conway?"

"Search is much too strong a word," he answered thoughtfully. "You can't really search a country half as big as Europe for one man. All I can say is that I visited places where I thought I might find him, or at least hear news of him. His last message, you remember, was that he had left Bangkok heading northwest. There were traces of him for a little way through the villages, and I think he probably made for the tribal regions along the Chinese border. He wouldn't have wanted to go through Burma—too many British officials who might have recognized him."

"You thought it might be easier to look for the valley of Blue Moon?"

"Well, it did seem like it might be a more fixed target. I suppose you read through that manuscript of mine?"

"Much more than read it. I should have returned it, but you left no address."

Rutherford nodded. "I wonder what you made of it?"

"I thought it remarkable—assuming, of course, that it's all genuinely based on what Conway told you."

"I give you my solemn word for that. I invented nothing at all—indeed, there's even less of my own language in it than you might think. Conway had a way of describing things that made them live, and don't forget that we had about twenty-four hours of practically continuous conversation."

"Well, as I said, it's all very remarkable."

He leaned back and smiled. "If that's all you're going to say, I can see I shall have to speak for myself. I suppose you consider me rather credulous. I don't really think I am. People make mistakes in life through believing too much, but they have a damned dull time if they believe too little. I was certainly taken with Conway's story—in more ways than one—and that was why I felt interested enough to follow as many clues as I could, apart from the chance of meeting the man himself."

He went on, after lighting a cigar: "It meant a good deal of odd journeying, but I like that sort of thing, and my publishers can't object to a travel book now and then. Altogether I must have covered some thousands of miles—Baskul, Bangkok, Chung-Kiang, Kashgar—I visited them all, and somewhere inside the area between them lies the heart of the mystery. But it's a pretty big area, you know, and all my investigations barely touched the edges of it."

"And Tibet?" I asked. "Did you find anything there?"

"My dear fellow, I never got into Tibet at all. The people at Government House wouldn't hear of it. It's as much as they'll do to sanction an Everest expedition, and when I said I thought of wandering about the Kun Luns on my own, they looked at me as if I'd suggested writing a biography of Gandhi. To be honest, they knew more than I did. Exploring Tibet isn't a one-man job; it needs a properly equipped expedition with someone who knows at least a few words of the language."

"Did you see the mountains at all?"

"I actually went as far as seeing them in the distance, on a very clear day—perhaps fifty miles off. Not many Europeans can claim even that. They looked just like a white line drawn across the horizon, that was all. In Yarkand and Kashgar I questioned everyone I met about them, but it was extraordinary how little I could discover. I should think they must be the least explored range in the world. I had the luck to meet an American who had once tried to cross them but hadn't been able to find a pass. He said there were passes, but they were incredibly high and completely unmapped. I asked if he thought it possible for a valley to exist of the kind Conway described, and he said he wouldn't call it impossible, but he thought it unlikely—on geological grounds, at least."

Then I asked if he had ever heard of a cone-shaped mountain almost as high as the highest of the Himalayas, and his answer was quite intriguing. There was a legend, he said, about such a mountain, but he thought there could be no truth to it. There were even rumors about peaks higher than Everest, but he didn't believe those either. 'I doubt if any peak in the Kun Luns is more than twenty-five thousand feet,' he said. But he admitted that they had never been properly surveyed.

"Then I asked him what he knew about Tibetan monasteries—he'd been in the country several times—and he gave me just the usual accounts that you can read in all the books. They weren't beautiful places, he assured me, and the monks in them were generally corrupt and dirty. 'Do they live long?' I asked, and he said yes, they often did, if they didn't die of some filthy disease. Then I went boldly to the point and asked if he'd ever heard legends of extreme longevity among the lamas. 'Heaps of them,' he answered. 'It's one of the stock tales you hear everywhere, but you can't verify them. You're told that some frightening-looking creature has been walled up in a cell for a hundred years, and he certainly looks as if he might have been, but of course you can't demand his birth certificate.'"

"Did the names 'Karakal' and 'Shangri-La' mean anything to him?"

"Not a thing. But he did tell me something interesting. He said he once told a fellow he met in Tibet that if he went out of his way at all, it would be to avoid monasteries, not visit them. That chance remark caught my attention, and I asked him when this meeting in Tibet had taken place. 'Oh, a long time ago,' he answered, 'before the War—in nineteen-eleven, I think it was.' He'd been traveling then for some American geographical society with several colleagues—a proper expedition, in fact. Somewhere near the Kun Luns they met this Chinese man being carried in a chair by native bearers. The fellow turned out to speak English quite well and strongly recommended they visit a certain monastery in the neighborhood—he even offered to guide them there. The American said they weren't interested and didn't have time, and that was that."

Rutherford paused. "I don't suggest it means a great deal. When a man tries to remember a casual incident that happened twenty years ago, you can't build too much on it. But it offers an interesting possibility."

"Yes, though if a well-equipped expedition had accepted the invitation, I don't see how they could have been detained at the monastery against their will."

"Quite true. And perhaps it wasn't Shangri-La at all."

We thought it over, but it seemed too vague for argument, and I went on to ask if there had been any discoveries at Baskul.

"Baskul was hopeless, and Peshawar was worse. Nobody would tell me anything except that the kidnapping of the airplane did undoubtedly take place. They weren't keen even to admit that—it's an episode they're not proud of. I verified, however, that it was capable of climbing high enough to cross the ranges. I also tried to trace Barnard, but I found his past history so mysterious that I wouldn't be surprised if he really were Chalmers Bryant, as Conway said."

"Did you try to find anything about the actual kidnapper?"

"I did, but again it was hopeless. The Air Force man whom the fellow had knocked out and impersonated had since been killed, so that promising line of inquiry was closed. I even wrote to a friend of mine in America who runs a flying school, asking if he had had any Tibetan pupils lately, but his reply was prompt and disappointing. He said he couldn't tell Tibetans from Chinese, and he had had about fifty of the latter—all training to fight the Japanese."

Rutherford paused to refill our glasses. "But I did make one rather curious discovery—and one which I could have made just as easily without leaving London. There was a German professor at Jena about the middle of the last century who took to globe-trotting and visited Tibet in 1887. He never came back, and there was some story about him having been drowned in fording a river. His name was Friedrich Meister."

"Good heavens—one of the names Conway mentioned!"

"Yes—though it may only have been coincidence. It doesn't prove the whole story, by any means, because the Jena fellow was born in 1845."

"But it's odd," I said.

"Oh yes, it's odd enough."

"Did you succeed in tracing any of the others?"

"No. It's a pity I hadn't a longer list to work on. I couldn't find any record of a pupil of Chopin's called Briac, though of course that doesn't prove that there wasn't one. Conway was pretty sparing with his names, when you come to think about it—out of fifty odd lamas supposed to be on the premises he only gave us one or two. Perrault and Henschell proved equally impossible to trace."

"How about Mallinson?" I asked. "Did you try to find out what had happened to him? And that girl—the Chinese girl?"

"My dear fellow, of course I did. The awkward part was, as you perhaps gathered from the manuscript, that Conway's story ended at the moment of leaving the valley with the porters. After that he either couldn't or wouldn't tell me what happened —perhaps he might have done, mind you, if there'd been more time. I feel that we can guess at some sort of tragedy. The hardships of the journey would have been perfectly appalling, apart from the risk of brigandage or even treachery among their own escorting party. Probably we shall never know exactly what did occur, but it seems tolerably certain that Mallinson never reached China. I made all sorts of inquiries, you know. First of all I tried to trace details of books sent in large consignments across the Tibetan frontier, but at all the likely places, such as Shanghai and Pekin, I drew complete blanks. That, of course, doesn't count for much, since the lamas would doubtless see that their methods of importation were kept secret. Then I tried at Tatsien-Fu. It's a weird place, a sort of world's-end market town, deuced difficult to get at, where the Chinese coolies from Yunnan transfer their loads of tea to the Tibetans. You can read about it in my new book when it comes out. Europeans don't often get as far. I found the people quite civil and courteous, but there was absolutely no record of Conway's party arriving at all."

"So how Conway himself reached Chung-Kiang is still unexplained?"

"The only conclusion is that he wandered there, just as he might have wandered anywhere else. Anyhow, we're back in the realm of hard facts when we get to Chung-Kiang, that's something. The nuns at the mission hospital were genuine enough, and so, for that matter, was Sieveking's excitement on the ship when Conway played that pseudo-Chopin." Rutherford paused and then added reflectively: "It's really an exercise in the balancing of probabilities, and I must say the scales don't bump very emphatically either way. Of course, if you don't accept Conway's story, it means that you doubt either his veracity or his sanity— one may as well be frank."

He paused again, as if inviting a comment, and I said: "As you know, I never saw him after the War, but I understand he was a good deal changed by it."

Rutherford answered: "Yes, he certainly was, there's no denying the fact. You can't subject a mere boy to three years of intense physical and emotional stress without tearing something to tatters. People would say, I suppose, that he came through without a scratch. But the scratches were there—on the inside."

We talked for a little time about the War and its effects on various people, and at length he went on: "But there's just one more point that I must mention—and perhaps in some ways the oddest of all. It came out during my inquiries at the mission. They all did their best for me there, as you can guess, but they couldn't recollect much, especially as they'd been so busy with a fever epidemic at the time. One of the questions I put was about the manner Conway had reached the hospital first of all —whether he had presented himself alone, or had been found ill and been taken there by someone else. They couldn't exactly remember—after all, it was a long while back—but suddenly, when I was on the point of giving up the cross-examination, one of the nuns remarked quite casually—'I think the doctor said he was brought here by a woman.' That was all she could tell me, and as the doctor himself had left the mission, there was no confirmation to be had on the spot.

"But having got so far, I wasn't in any mood to give up. It appeared that the doctor had gone to a bigger hospital in Shanghai, so I took the trouble to get his address and call on him there. It was just after the Jap air-raiding, and things were pretty grim. I'd met the man before during my first visit to Chung-Kiang, and he was very polite, though terribly overworked—yes, terribly's the word, for, believe me, the air-raids on London by the Germans were just nothing to what the Japs did to the native parts of Shanghai. Oh yes, he said instantly, he remembered the case of the Englishman who had lost his memory. Was it true he had been brought to the mission hospital by a woman? I asked. Oh yes, certainly, by a woman, a Chinese woman. Did he remember anything about her? Nothing, he answered, except that she had been ill of the fever herself, and had died almost immediately... Just then there was an interruption—a batch of wounded were carried in and packed on stretchers in the corridors—the wards were all full—and I didn't care to go on taking up the man's time, especially as the thudding of the guns at Woosung was a reminder that he would still have plenty to do. When he came back to me, looking quite cheerful even amidst such ghastliness, I just asked him one final question, and I dare say you can guess what it was. 'About that Chinese woman,' I said. 'Was she young?'"

Rutherford flicked his cigar as if the narration had excited him quite as much as he hoped it had me. Continuing, he said: "The little fellow looked at me solemnly for a moment, and then answered in that funny clipped English that the educated Chinese have—'Oh no, she was most old—most old of anyone I have ever seen.'"

We sat for a long time in silence, and then talked again of Conway as I remembered him, boyish and gifted and full of charm, and of the War that had altered him, and of so many mysteries of time and age and of the mind, and of the little Manchu who had been "most old," and of the strange ultimate dream of Blue Moon. "Do you think he will ever find it?" I asked.

Rutherford answered, with the gentlest of smiles: "I wouldn't be surprised. After all, there must be places that time has missed - corners of the world where wisdom and beauty still survive. And if anyone could find such a place again, it would be Conway." He looked thoughtful. "It's comforting to think that somewhere, even now, he might be climbing those tremendous mountains, searching for that hidden valley."

"And if he finds it?"

"Then perhaps the world still has its Shangri-Las - its sacred places where time moves differently and the best of human wisdom is kept safe." He smiled again. "We need such places, even if we can only dream about them."

As my train pulled out of Delhi the next morning, I found myself looking up at the distant mountains and wondering if somewhere beyond them, in a valley that time had forgotten, Conway had found his way home at last.

JAMES HILTON

ACKNOWLEDGMENTS

First and foremost, I must acknowledge James Hilton, whose creation of Shangri-La has captured readers' imaginations for nearly a century. His vision of a place where wisdom and beauty could survive the storms of history seems even more relevant today than when he first wrote it.

This adaptation owes much to the many scholars and explorers who have documented the real mysteries of Tibet and the Himalayas. Their accounts of hidden valleys, ancient monasteries, and remarkable discoveries helped me understand the world that Conway entered.

To my friends in China who helped me understand the subtle beauties of Chinese culture, art, and music that play such an important role in this story - thank you for your patience with my endless questions.

To my editors, who helped me find the delicate balance between preserving Hilton's philosophical depths and making them accessible to modern readers - your guidance was invaluable.

To my family, who never complained when I disappeared into my own version of Shangri-La while working on this project - thank you for understanding that some journeys must be made alone, even if only in imagination.

And finally, to all readers who pick up this book: may you find in Conway's journey what generations before you have found - that there are still mysteries in the world, that wisdom and beauty are worth preserving, and that sometimes the most incredible discoveries come when we stop rushing and simply listen to the quiet voice of time.

J.C.S.

Wiesbaden
February 8th, 2025